D0866871

Chicago Public Library
Oriole Park Branch
7454 W. Balmoral Ave.
Chicago, IL 60656

Swept Up

by Suzanne Harper

d on the series created by Michael Poryes and Rich Correll & Barry O'Brien

Disney Press
New York

R0421570802

Oriole Park Branch
7454 W. Balmoral Ave.
Chicago, IL 60656
312-744-1965
Mon-Thur 9-9
Fri & Sat 9-5; Sun Closed

Hannah Montana

Swept Up

For Elizabeth Rudnick,
with thanks for everything.

Copyright © 2009 Disney Enterprises, Inc.
All rights reserved. Published by Disney Press, an imprint of Disney
Book Group. No part of this book may be reproduced or transmitted
in any form or by any means, electronic or mechanical, including
photocopying, recording, or by any information storage and retrieval system,
without written permission from the publisher. For information address
Disney Press, 114 Fifth Avenue, New York, New York 10011-5690.

Printed in the United States of America
First Edition
1 3 5 7 9 10 8 6 4 2

Library of Congress Control Number on file.
ISBN 978-1-4231-2091-9

For more Disney Press fun, visit www.disneybooks.com
Visit DisneyChannel.com

Reinforced binding

Designed by Roberta Pressel

SUSTAINABLE
FORESTRY
INITIATIVE

Certified Fiber
Sourcing

www.sfiprogram.org

THIS LABEL APPLIES TO TEXT STOCK

 *Chapter One*

Come get your duds in order,
For we're going to leave tomorrow,
Heave away, me jollies, heave away.
                    —"Heave Away"

As her private jet circled in the sky, fifteen-year-old Miley Stewart stared through a window at the island of Nantucket below. It looked like an emerald suspended between the blue waters of the Atlantic and the cloudless blue summer sky.

She felt her heart lift with excitement as she thought of the week that lay ahead: swimming in the surf, bike riding through charming island towns, having picnics on the beach. . . .

Miley sighed happily, her bright eyes sparkling with anticipation. "We are going to have so much fun," she said.

Her best friend, Lilly Truscott, leaned over to try to see out the window as well. "You got that right," she said. Lilly was so excited she was bouncing in her seat. Her neatly braided blond hair bounced, too. "Hey, I have an idea! We should rent surfboards while we're here. I've heard the Atlantic waves are killer."

Oliver Oken's head popped up over the back of Miley's and Lilly's seats. "Excuse me for being the voice of reason here," he said. "But I don't think any sport that uses the word 'killer' is a sport that I want to participate in. How about we just kick back on the beach instead of risking our lives in the water?"

"Why not do both?" Lilly asked in a reasonable voice. "Risk our lives in the morning, kick back in the afternoon. It's the perfect schedule."

"Perfect if you don't care about going home in one piece," Oliver said, brushing his brown bangs out of his face. "Me, I'm going to work on my tan."

"And maybe do a little shopping," Miley added. "Oh, we've totally got to go on a boat ride, too—"

"Hold on now." Across the aisle, Miley's father, Robby Ray Stewart, glanced up from the spy novel he was reading. "Remember, *Miley* may be on vacation, but *Hannah's* got a job to do."

Miley sank back into her seat and sighed. "I know, I remember," she said.

Maintaining two different identities was hard sometimes, but she was used to it. As Miley Stewart, she was just an average Malibu high school student who struggled with math and got crushes on boys. But as Hannah Montana, she was a famous pop star who gave concerts around the world and was interviewed by major magazines and on TV shows.

She and her dad had decided long ago that they would keep her identity as Hannah Montana a secret so she could enjoy a regular life when she wasn't performing. It had been a smart decision, she thought. She wouldn't have become friends with Lilly and Oliver—such good friends that she had finally told them her secret—if she had stayed inside the celebrity bubble.

But it did mean that she often had to live in two completely different worlds at the same time. This vacation, for example, had been made possible by *Entertainment Insider* magazine. The editor had wanted to do a "homespun, completely casual" photo shoot with Hannah Montana using the quaint cottages of Nantucket as a backdrop. The magazine had even paid for the private plane they were flying in. The only downside was . . .

"I'm going have to use my best 'presto change-o' moves to keep everybody from figuring out my secret," Miley said, thinking out loud.

"Oh, you don't need to worry about that," said Roxy, Hannah's bodyguard. She had been doing slow-motion martial arts moves in the aisle for the last thirty minutes, claiming that she needed to keep limber in case an overeager photographer tried to jump them at the airport. "Remember, Roxy's got your back. No one's gonna know anything about Hannah Montana that we don't want them to know."

Miley's older brother, Jackson, let out a small snort. "Yeah, like the fact that she has serious morning breath," he said. "We're talking grizzly-bear breath. After a long winter of hibernation."

"Daaddd!" Miley cried. "Make him stop."

"Sorry, bud," Mr. Stewart said, going back to his book. "I am officially on vacation. No work, no worries, and absolutely no acting as a referee. You two will have to sort things out yourselves."

Jackson grinned, his green eyes alight with mischief as he continued to needle his sister. "Oh, yeah, I could totally give *Entertainment Insider* a big scoop if I wanted to," he went on. "I bet they'd be interested in knowing that Hannah Montana cuts her toenails in the bathtub, eats peanut butter right out of the jar, and never makes her bed. Not to mention—"

"Hey, Roxy," Miley said, giving her brother a menacing stare, "I think you need to practice that judo hold you were talking about. The one where you twist a certain person's arm behind his back until he screams like a little girl."

"Sorry," Roxy said, "I'm saving that move for someone who's *real* trouble." She slashed her hands through the air a couple of times. "Hi-*ya!*"

Her plan foiled, Miley pointedly turned her back on her brother and addressed Lilly. "I'm so glad it worked out that you and Oliver could come with us on our vacation," she said.

"Me, too," Lilly said. "Even though I did have to sign up for a summer-school class to get my mom to let me take the trip *and* promise to stay with a great-aunt I barely know."

Lilly's great-aunt lived on Nantucket. As soon as Lilly had heard about Miley's trip, she had jumped on the Internet. A little research turned up a class in sailing navigation that would give Lilly extra math credits. That, plus the knowledge that Lilly would be staying with family, convinced Lilly's mom to let her go.

And since Oliver desperately needed math credits—and since his mother was planning to redecorate the upstairs bathroom, which would be much easier with him out of the house—he had been included as well.

"You could have stayed at the cottage Dad rented," Miley said.

Lilly shrugged. "You know how Mom is. She was worried that I would be taking advantage of your hospitality. And she was pretty psyched that I would get a chance to get to know Great-aunt Agatha better." Lilly's face clouded. "I just hope it's not too weird. I mean, the last time I saw her, I was six months old! It's really like staying with a stranger. And Mom said she's kind of eccentric—"

"I think it'll be cool," Oliver said. "Come on, your great-aunt is a best-selling mystery writer!"

Lilly just shrugged. "I'm not that into mysteries."

"How can you not want to read a book like this?" Oliver held up a paperback called *Murder Most Maniacal.* The illustration on the cover showed a woman running away from a dark, looming mansion, a look of terror on her face. "It's great. I'm only up to chapter five, and already two people have been murdered. Everyone thinks the killer is a long-lost cousin who came back to town just in time to stake his claim on an inheritance, but I think it's the gardener. He's always lurking."

"Oh, that's a big clue right there," Roxy

agreed. "That's how you know someone's a bad guy. All the lurking."

At that moment, the pilot announced that everybody should take their seats. Roxy sat down, fastened her seat belt, and pulled a clipboard out of her big bag. "All right, let's get organized," she said. "Lilly, after we pick up the car, we'll drop you and Oliver off at your great-aunt's. Then we'll go to the supermarket and get food for the week. Then we'll go to the beach house and drop off Mr. Stewart and Jackson."

"Eee, doggie," Mr. Stewart said, grinning. "I'm sure glad you could come with us, Roxy. With you in charge, this is going to be a real vacation for me. First one I've had in years." He got a dreamy look in his eyes. "All I'm going to be doin' is sitting on the beach, watching the waves, and maybe writing a song or two."

"Yes, sir," Roxy said. "You don't need to worry about a thing, 'cause you got Roxy to act as bodyguard, referee, and general commander-in-chief of this little expedition. So, like I was saying, first, we drop Lilly and Oliver off at her great-aunt's. Then, once we get to the beach house, Miley, you'll need to change into Hannah right away. Then it's on to the Bumblebee Inn where we'll be staying—"

"What?" Miley turned to her. "Already? I thought the photo shoot was going to start tomorrow. I thought maybe we could chill at the house."

"That's true," Roxy replied. "But those magazine folks know that Hannah flew in today. They might get suspicious if you don't check in until tomorrow." She tapped her temple. "See, Roxy's always thinking. Once we've checked in, I'll establish a perimeter, sweep our rooms for listening devices, and look around for hidden cameras."

Miley sighed. "Fine," she said. "But I thought we were supposed to be on vacation. I thought we were going to relax."

"We *will* relax," Roxy assured her. "In between Hannah Montana's photo shoot for *Entertainment Insider* magazine and Lilly and Oliver's summer-school classes and my bodyguard duties, we will be relaxing like all get-out."

"Ooh, yeah, sounds like you guys will really be kicking back," Jackson said. "Not like me and Dad. Our schedule is going to be superbusy: sleep until noon, eat breakfast, hang out on the beach, eat lunch, take a nap. . . ."

"We got it, we got it—your idea of a vacation is behaving like a lazy slug," Miley snapped. "Oh, wait! That's the way you act in your *regular* life."

As the plane descended, Miley turned back to the window and began to daydream again. Even though she had to be Hannah Montana for part of the time, she hoped that there would still be plenty of time to be Miley. And plenty of opportunities to have fun.

Chapter Two

Come all-ye young fellows that follow the sea,
To my way, haye, blow man down,
And pray pay attention and listen to me,
Give me some time to blow the man down.
                    —"Blow the Man Down"

It took longer than usual to collect their bags, thanks to the extra suitcases Miley had to bring along to carry all her Hannah clothes and makeup.

"This is so typical," Jackson complained as he wheeled a luggage cart over to the baggage carousel. "I still can't believe you have a special case just for your wigs!"

"What can I say?" Miley replied sweetly.

"Hannah Montana has a stylin' fashion rep to uphold."

Jackson shook his head as he heaved a particularly large suitcase onto the cart. "I'd hate to see how you'd handle being stranded on a desert island, Miss Hannah."

But he cheered up when they got to the parking lot and he saw the fancy car that was waiting for them. It was black, sleek, and very cool.

"I'm driving!" Jackson said immediately.

Miley, Lilly, and Oliver exchanged uneasy glances, but only Miley was willing to speak up.

"Uh-uh, no way," Miley said. "This is supposed to be a relaxing vacation, remember? And the first rule about relaxing is, don't get into a car accident before you've left the parking lot."

"I don't think I like what you're implying," Jackson said with a cold look. "I happen to be an excellent driver."

"Yeah, tell that to the garage door," Miley

said. "Or the fire hydrant on the corner. Or—"

"You're taking every incident completely out of context," Jackson said. "And you're ignoring all the times I *didn't* hit something."

"All right, enough bickering," Roxy said, tossing the car keys to Jackson. "Nantucket's a slow-paced kinda place, from what I understand. I think Jackson can handle driving our car—"

"Thank you, Roxy," Jackson said, casting a smug look at Miley.

"As long as I sit right next to you," Roxy said. "That way I can yell in your ear if I see an accident about to happen. Oliver, you think you can handle that bad boy?" she asked, nodding toward a particularly large suitcase.

"Sure, no problem," Oliver said. "You know, I've been working out," he added, raising his arm and flexing his bicep.

He managed to shift the suitcase to the lip of the trunk, but as soon as he tried to lift it, he lost his balance and teetered backward.

"Okay," he said weakly as he lay flat on his back with the suitcase on top of him. "Maybe it's a slight problem. . . ."

Roxy rolled her eyes, then picked up the suitcase and lifted it into the trunk as if it weighed nothing. "Nothing ever changes," she muttered to herself. "Roxy's always gotta do everything."

Once they had the luggage stowed, Miley and Lilly got in the backseat along with Mr. Stewart. Jackson slid into the driver's seat and Roxy scooted into the passenger side, followed by Oliver and his trusty map.

"Oops, sorry," Oliver said as he unfolded the map right in Roxy's face.

It took him several attempts to get the map under control, but he finally managed to fold it into a manageable size. "Let's see," he said as he studied it. "This little arrow shows where we are right now, in the parking lot of the airport, which means that this little line is the road . . . and here's the town, but it looks like this road is going the other way. . . . Oh, wait, I think I have this thing upside down—"

"For heaven's sake, boy," Roxy snapped. "Give me that." She snatched the map from Oliver's hands, turned it right-side up, and handed it back to him. "It's a good thing you are taking a navigation class on this little trip. I've never seen anyone get lost as easily as you do."

"I'm never lost," Oliver protested. "After all, wherever I go . . . there I am."

Roxy thought about that for a moment, opened her mouth as if to argue, then shook her head. "Whatever you say, Buddha Boy," she said.

Oliver had already turned back to the map and was studying it intensely. "Okay! It looks like all we have to do is turn down this red line, then hang a left after the little blue squiggle."

"You got it!" Jackson said. He pulled out of the parking lot with a lurch and a peal of tires.

By the time they reached the main road,

Miley and Lilly were clutching each other's hands, and Mr. Stewart's eyes were squeezed shut. Ten minutes later, after swerving to avoid a branch in the road, bumping over a curb, and screeching to a stop at a red light, even Roxy looked as if her famous self-control might desert her.

"Boy, you are a menace on the road," Mr. Stewart said from the backseat. "Remind me never to let you borrow my car again once we get home."

"*If* we get home," Lilly muttered from where she was huddled next to Miley.

"What are you guys complaining about?" Jackson yelled breezily over his shoulder. "Just because I drive with a certain panache—"

"Watch out!" Oliver screamed.

"Whoa!" Jackson slammed on the brakes when he realized that he was going the wrong way down a one-way street. Horns blared as he backed up, waving apologetically to the other drivers.

"How about a little less panache and a little more paying attention to clearly marked road signs?" Roxy suggested sarcastically.

"There's no room for style in this world anymore," Jackson muttered, but he drove more sedately down another street. This one ran along the waterfront. A row of wooden four-masted ships, their white sails snapping in the breeze, were anchored just offshore. The road meandered along the coastline for several more miles and, as they drove on, the houses began to get farther and farther apart. Finally, they found themselves following a narrow road high above the ocean.

"Here we are," Jackson said proudly. "Four twenty-three Nightbird Lane."

They all stared at the sign displaying the house's address. It was a metal sculpture of a flying owl. The owl was holding a mouse in its beak. And the mouse was holding a plaque with the house number on it.

"Wow," Oliver said as they all piled out of

the car. "This looks *exactly* like the kind of place where Agatha Kilpatrick, the author of *We Wish You a Merry Murder*, would live."

Lilly stared up at the gray Victorian house. It was set on a bluff high over the sea; waves crashed on rocks just behind the house. The salty air had weathered the paint; much of it was faded and peeling. The front lawn was overgrown and weedy, and a single shutter creaked in the breeze.

Suddenly the front door flew open and a tall, thin woman swept out onto the porch, down the steps, and along the path to greet them. She wore a long, filmy gray dress that almost seemed to be made of cobwebs. Her iron-gray hair was pulled back into a severe bun. She peered at them through round, steel-rimmed glasses.

Then she smiled—a thin, pointed smile, that was shaped like a capital *V.* Her voice, when she finally spoke, was spiky.

"Ah, my great-niece Lilly," she said. "At

last. I am your great-aunt Agatha." She held out her hand to Lilly.

"Hello," Lilly said a bit tentatively.

"So, which of these two young men is your friend Oliver?" Mrs. Kilpatrick asked. Her wintry gaze rested on Jackson for a moment.

Jackson gulped. "He is," Jackson said, pushing Oliver in front of him.

Oliver stumbled, caught himself, then recovered enough to smile charmingly at the older woman.

"Oliver Oken, ma'am," he said. "Pleased to meet you. Thank you for having me . . ." He searched his mind for the other polite phrases his mother had drilled into him before he had left on this trip. "I hope I won't be too much trouble."

Mrs. Kilpatrick flashed another smile. "I'm sure you won't," she said. Then she added in a steely voice, "Because I don't tolerate trouble. Of any sort."

Oliver blinked at this response, just as a

black cat slipped through the long grass to sit at Mrs. Kilpatrick's feet.

She looked down.

The cat looked up.

Their eyes met.

Then Mrs. Kilpatrick gave a slow nod, and the cat jumped up and ran to the porch.

"That's Marlowe," she said. "He will show you to your rooms."

"He . . . he will?" Lilly asked.

Mrs. Kilpatrick smiled. "Yes, you'll find he's quite bright. All cats are, of course, but Marlowe is exceptionally intelligent. Now, I'm sure you have some suitcases, yes?"

As Roxy helped them take their bags out of the trunk of the car, Oliver whispered to Lilly, "I'm not feeling too good about this. Did you see the way Marlowe seemed to read her mind?"

"Don't be ridiculous," Lilly said. But she sounded uneasy. "She was just teasing us, that's all."

Roxy patted her arm. "Don't you worry about your aunt Agatha. Remember, I know twelve kinds of martial arts if you need help." She winked. "Including a special cat karate."

Lilly and Oliver relaxed enough to grin.

"Thanks," Lilly said. "I'm sure we'll be fine."

As Lilly hauled her suitcase through the gate to the front walkway, Oliver leaned close to Roxy. "Keep your cell phone on. Just in case," he whispered.

 *Chapter Three*

Blow ye winds westerly, blow ye winds, blow,
Jolly sou'wester, boys, steady she goes.
                              —"The Fish of the Sea"

The next morning dawned clear and bright. Miley blinked, then turned to look at the bedside clock. She was astonished to see that it was only 6:30. She never got up this early—or, at least, she never got up this early unless she absolutely had to, and then she did so with much grumbling and protest.

But she felt surprisingly awake and alert. After a moment, she realized the reason for this. Though the window was covered by a shade, there was a transom at the top that let the sunlight into the room. Miley jumped up and went over to the window to peek out.

Seagulls floated in the vaulting blue sky. A square-rigger ship, its white sails billowing, moved grandly from the harbor out to sea. The smell of cinnamon buns and coffee wafted in through the window on a gentle breeze. She was on vacation!

Miley bounded into the bathroom. The photo shoot wasn't scheduled to begin for another hour or so, but she couldn't wait to start the day. After a hot shower, she spent some time applying her makeup and was just putting on her Hannah wig when there was a gentle knock at her bedroom door.

Three taps. Then one. Then two.

Miley grinned. Roxy loved coming up with code names and secret knocks and special hand signals. Miley got up to open the door.

"Mornin', Roxy," she said. "When did you get up?"

Roxy didn't answer. Instead, she frowned and asked, "What do you think you're doing, just opening the door like that? What happened to, 'Who's there?'"

Miley stood aside as her bodyguard pushed her way into the room after one or two suspicious looks up and down the hall. "I didn't think I had to ask 'who's there,' since you used our special knock," Miley protested. "I mean, what's the point of a secret knock if it's not to let you know that the person who's knocking is a person who knows the secret knock. . . ." Her voice trailed off in confusion. "Oh, you know what I mean."

"I do, and I keep telling you, there's no such thing as too much security," Roxy said. She looked at the window curtains, which were now pulled back, then eyed Miley. "And I hope you got Hannah'd up before you let anyone with twenty-twenty vision get a glimpse of you through that window."

Miley rolled her eyes. "Of course I did,"

she said. "I didn't just fall off the back of the tour bus, you know."

There was another knock on the door. Miley turned to open it, but Roxy dived in front of Miley and turned to face her, her back against the door.

"What did I just tell you?" she demanded.

"*Sor*-ry," Miley said.

"It wasn't even the secret knock this time!" Roxy scolded. She looked through the peephole. "Who is it?"

"Room service," said a voice from the hall.

Roxy narrowed her eyes. "Let me see that breakfast tray." She waited until the waiter took the silver cover off a plate of pancakes to prove his identity. After taking a long look, she nodded and opened the door.

He pushed the cart inside. "Good morning," he said brightly, reaching for the silver cover on a dish. "Here's your—*aaggh*!"

Roxy had pushed him against the wall and was patting him down.

"What are you doing?" Miley said.

"Checking for secret cameras and hidden tape recorders," Roxy said briefly. "Can't be too careful." She stepped back from the waiter, who was huddled fearfully in the corner. "Okay, sir. You're good to go."

He held out the bill with a trembling hand. "If you'd just sign this . . ."

Roxy signed, and he fled.

"Roxy! I know you're my bodyguard, but come on," Miley scolded. "That poor guy was shaking."

"Can't be too careful," Roxy said. "And I promised your daddy I'd have your back. You know what that means? Every minute of every hour of every day, I am looking out for your best interests. Protecting you. Keeping you safe. Making sure—"

"That sinister waiters are kept at bay," Miley finished, taking a bite of pancake. "I got it."

She finished her breakfast quickly, mindful of the magazine crew waiting downstairs.

Then, with one last check of her makeup, Miley headed for the door.

Once again, Roxy moved fast and blocked her way.

"Hold on there, honey," Roxy said. "Let me check out the perimeter first." She opened the door and stuck her head out. She looked right and left. Then she waved for Miley to follow her.

"All right," Roxy said as she opened the door wider. "Go, go, go!"

"Why do I always feel like I'm in an action movie when I'm with you?" Miley asked. Then she slipped into the hallway, Roxy right behind her.

"Hannah Montana! So pleased to meet you!" A man with short dark hair and a goatee jumped up from his chair as Miley and Roxy entered the lobby of the Bumblebee Inn.

"I'm Jeremy Simple, the art director for *Entertainment Insider,*" the man said, peering at them through his horn-rimmed glasses. He pointed to another man with spiky blond hair who was carrying a camera. "And that's Chad Mackey, our photographer." He waved vaguely toward two girls sitting in the corner. "Josie does hair and makeup. Sabrina is our stylist."

Miley smiled politely as everyone exchanged hellos. "Thanks. It's nice to meet y'all. This is my bodyguard, Roxy."

Jeremy raised one eyebrow in surprise. "But Nantucket is so quiet and peaceful. Do you really think a bodyguard is necessary?"

"Oh, Roxy is more than necessary," Roxy said, folding her arms and narrowing her eyes. "Roxy is *essential.* And Roxy doesn't ever let her guard down—even on Nantucket."

She locked eyes with Jeremy, who had to look away within seconds. "Yes, of course, absolutely, whatever will make you comfortable, Hannah!" he said. "Now, we've picked a few locations to use for the next few days, but we thought we'd start with Main Street. This is such a charming small town—"

"Total Americana," Chad agreed, nodding. "We'll show you window-shopping, getting an ice-cream cone, maybe flying a kite."

"Sounds good," Miley said. "I know y'all probably brought tons of clothes for the shoot, but I thought since you wanted to show the *real* me that maybe you'd want to take pictures of me in my own clothes."

Jeremy began walking slowly around Hannah, squinting as he looked her up and down. "Mmm," he said. "Interesting thought. But I'm not sure the outfit you have on is *quite* the way we want to go. What do you think, Chad?"

Chad looked through his camera's view-finder, then shook his head. "Nope," he said. "*Way* too casual."

"What?" Miley looked down at what she was wearing: floral cotton shorts, a crisp white blouse, sandals . . . "I thought this shoot was *supposed* to be casual. I thought the idea was to show the down-home Hannah."

Jeremy put a hand on Miley's arm and

smiled reassuringly. "Oh, yes, that was the original idea," he said. "But our editor just got the results of our most recent reader survey, and guess what? It turns out that people want celebrities to look like celebrities! I mean, what's the point of buying a magazine to read about someone who's just like us, right?"

"I guess so," Miley said.

Jeremy stared through narrowed eyes at Miley, thoughtfully stroking his goatee. Then he called out, "Josie! Sabrina!" and snapped his fingers. The two girls scurried over. They looked like twins: both petite, with pixie haircuts and several earrings in each ear. The only difference was that Josie's hair was purple and Sabrina's was pink.

Josie reached out to touch Miley's blond Hannah wig. "Maybe we should curl this?" she suggested. "For a different look?"

"No!" Miley said, panicked. "I mean, I like it long and straight. And that's what my fans expect."

Josie sighed heavily. "Fine. I'll just redo your makeup, then," she said. "Make it a little more dramatic."

Sabrina tilted her head to one side as she looked Miley up and down. "I can totally see you in a miniskirt and cute stiletto heels," she said. "With a funky necklace, a dozen bangle bracelets, some dangly earrings—you'll look adorable!"

"Really?" Miley was trying not to sound as nervous as she felt. "You don't think it will look a little . . . over-the-top for a summer afternoon in Nantucket?"

"Remember our survey," Jeremy said. "You are a celebrity, Hannah Montana! And you must always look like one!"

"Well . . . okay," Miley said. Then she trailed after Sabrina and Josie to begin her transformation.

Two hours later, Miley tottered onto the cobblestoned street outside the inn, blinking in the sunlight. She was wearing scarlet satin shoes with three-inch heels, a blue linen skirt, and a white silk blouse, plus a star-spangled scarf and an enormous straw hat.

"You look fantastic! Red, white, and blue, baby! Couldn't be more patriotic!" Chad cried out, snapping off a few quick shots. "Now try walking down the block toward that book-store."

"Sure," Miley said bravely, though *try* was the key word in that sentence, she thought. She was having a hard time just standing up!

Still, she took two tiny steps. She smiled, feeling a moment of triumph. *Yessss!* I didn't even fall!

And then she tried a third step and immediately lost her balance. After several nervous seconds of teetering back and forth and flailing her arms, she managed to stay upright, but her hat fell forward over her face, blocking her vision.

"That's good, keep walking," Chad said,

sounding encouraging. "Ignore me. Pretend I'm not here."

Yeah, that'll be easy, Miley thought. Considering I can't even *see* you.

She took a deep breath, pushed her hat out of her face, and started off once more. This time she made it halfway down the block before a gray and white terrier ran yapping across her path, knocking her over.

"Aagghh!" she cried.

"Pop star down! Pop star down!" Roxy yelled as she raced to Miley's rescue.

"This is terrible!" Miley muttered as Roxy helped her to her feet. "I'm going to look like the biggest klutz in the world to all the readers of *Entertainment Insider* magazine!"

Roxy brushed her off. "Now, honey, don't worry so much. Camera Boy back there's already taken a couple of hundred pictures. There's gotta be at least one where you look semicoordinated."

Miley sighed. She shouldn't have been

surprised. Her nickname in gym class was "Stinky Stewart," thanks to her total lack of athletic ability. That was why she loved dancing on the stage as Hannah Montana—it was the only time she felt graceful.

"Just take it slow, that's Roxy's advice." Her bodyguard took a long look at Miley's shoes and shook her head. "*Reeaaalll* slow. Those things they put on your feet look like more like stilts than shoes."

Chad walked up just in time to overhear this. "But they'll be fabulous in the photos," he assured Miley. "And they're incredibly fashion-forward!"

Then Jeremy joined them, frowning. "Did you get anything we can use?" he asked Chad. "Anything at all?"

In response, Chad held out his camera so Jeremy could see the photo display and quickly scrolled through the images.

"No, she's not smiling . . . right eye looks weird . . . hair's in her face . . . awkward pose . . . Oh, there's the trip . . . and the fall . . . that's terrible . . ." Jeremy muttered as the images flashed by.

"Excuse me? Hello?" Miley said. "I'm standing right here."

But Jeremy didn't seem to hear her. "Maybe we should sit her down somewhere," he told Chad. "Maybe it would be safer if we didn't ask her to move."

Now Miley was getting mad. "Hey," she said, leaning forward and waving a hand in front of them. "You do know I can hear every word—*aagghh*!"

For the second time that day, Miley lost her balance, pitched over . . . and landed in a large planter filled with petunias.

She looked up to see Jeremy and Chad staring down at her in surprise.

"Are you thinking what I'm thinking?" Jeremy asked Chad.

"Yep." Chad lifted his camera and fired off a dozen shots. "Photo op."

"Sweet niblets!" Miley yelled. "Get me out of here."

An hour later, Miley had eaten an ice-cream cone as Hannah Montana . . . and ended up with a blob of chocolate-vanilla swirl all over her face when she had tripped over the curb.

She had picked up a book from a table outside a bookstore . . . and managed to knock a bronze paperweight off the table and onto her toe.

She had also posed next to an artist who had set up her easel on the street . . . and managed to hit the canvas so that it fell to the ground.

When she got to the gallery that sold blown-glass ornaments and vases, however, Roxy decided it was time to call a halt to the tour of Main Street.

"Honey, you are going to single-handedly get Nantucket declared a disaster area," she said to Miley. "Your new nickname is going to be Hurricane Hannah. For generations to come, people are going to be telling stories about how you were hit with the klutz curse—"

"Yes, thanks, all right, I got it!" Miley snapped, fanning herself with her hat.

Josie and Sabrina stepped up, looking concerned. "Oh, no, your makeup is melting all over your face," Josie said, clucking her tongue. She pulled out a compact. "Let's see if I can fix that."

"And you look so hot and messy," Sabrina added, reaching into a bag for another white cotton blouse identical to the one Miley was wearing. "I think you should change. Jeremy just *hates* it when models have sweat stains on their clothes."

"Great," Miley muttered. "Anybody else want to damage my self-esteem? I'm standing by to take your calls."

As Josie freshened up her makeup, Miley noticed Jeremy and Chad looking in a store window. Their expressions were very intense as they talked and nodded to each other.

As soon as Josie was finished, Miley walked over to them . . . or rather, she inched her way over, trying her best not to trip, stumble, or catch a heel in between any menacing cobblestones.

"Hey, guys," she said brightly. "What's next?"

"I just had a great idea for a way to end today's shoot," Jeremy replied. He nodded toward the shop window. It was filled with huge, brightly colored kites. "How about we buy one of those kites—no, we'll ask the owner to give us one in return for mentioning the store in the magazine—and have you fly it down there on the docks? Boats in the background, a breeze blowing your hair, a pink and purple kite flying against the blue sky . . ."

Miley's smile quickly disappeared. "Um, I don't know," she said. "I'm not really in a kite-flying mood. . . ."

But Jeremy, as usual, wasn't listening. He made a square with the thumb and forefinger of each hand, as if to frame the vision, and peered through it. "Gorgeous! It might even be the cover shot!"

Miley bit her lip. "It's been a while since I've flown a kite," she confessed. "I'm not sure I'd be any good at it. . . ."

"How hard can it be?" Jeremy asked briskly. "Children do it every day."

A few moments later, Miley was standing on the docks with Roxy, holding the kite and waiting for Chad to finish checking his light meter and signal that he was ready to start shooting. Josie and Sabrina had been given the job of clearing the dock of tourists so that Miley would have room to fly her kite. Once they realized that the person being photographed was Hannah Montana, everyone left good-naturedly enough, especially since she signed autographs for anyone who wanted one.

Now, as Miley waited, she eased one foot out of her shoe and wiggled her toes. "Oh, that feels good." She sighed. "I can't wait to put my sneakers on."

She glanced across the water at the boats bobbing up and down. Many were sailboats or small motorboats, but one was a magnificent wooden sailing ship with a towering series of sails. It looked like the kind of ship that might have sailed out of Nantucket harbor two centuries ago in search of whales and high adventure.

As she watched, a sudden gust of wind made the sails billow. A teenage boy with sun-lightened brown hair ran nimbly along the railing to grab a rope. Miley squinted against the sun as she tried to follow his movements. He seemed to know what he was doing, she thought, as if the ship were his home. . . .

"Uh-uh, honey." Roxy's voice interrupted her thoughts. "I see what you're looking at."

"What?" Miley asked. "I just think that's a beautiful ship."

"Right," Roxy said dryly.

"And, um, historical," Miley added. "You know how much I love history."

"I remember how you whined for days about writing that essay on the Founding Fathers during your last tour," Roxy said. "I know what you're thinking about, girl, and it's not history."

"Come on, Roxy, I can't work every single minute," Miley pleaded. "I want to have *some* fun on this trip."

"Oh, you will, baby." Roxy patted her arm. "You'll have fun swimming with Oliver and shopping with Lilly and hanging out every minute of every day with me, your ever-lovin' bodyguard, who is paid to keep you out of trouble."

"I don't know why you think that every boy is trouble," Miley said.

Roxy gave her a level stare, the one that the Stewart family called "Roxy's ray-gun gaze." "Do we have to have another talk about boys and their rascally ways?" she asked. "'Cause I'd be glad to set aside an hour or two to explain to you—"

"No, no, that's all right, thank you anyway," Miley said hastily. The last time Roxy had lectured her about rascally boys, she'd ended up keeping Miley under strict—as in, "following Miley with a walkie-talkie" strict—surveillance for a month.

Just then, Sabrina came running up, holding the kite. "Chad told me to tell you he's ready," she said breathlessly. She thrust the kite into Miley's hands. "Okay, you know how to work this thing, right?"

"Uh, yeah, I think so," Miley answered. "You get the kite in the air, it catches a breeze, it flies. Right?"

"Don't ask me. I just buy the props, I don't know how to use them," Sabrina said with a shrug. "Anyway, Chad told me to tell you to run down the dock toward him, okay?" Miley nodded, and the stylist backed away.

"I guess I better get out of the way, too," Roxy said. "They don't want *me* in this photo shoot, that's for sure."

She hurried off, leaving Miley and the kite all alone. Miley looked down at the kite. "I sure hope this works," she muttered. Then she flashed a big smile in Chad's direction, tossed the kite in the air, and started running. . . .

This was, of course, destined to go horribly wrong. And it did.

Miley got the kite in the air after only three tries. That gave her confidence. But then, just as she started jogging toward Chad, she felt the kite dip. "Run faster, Hannah!" Jeremy hollered. "Go, go, go!"

Obediently, Miley tried to run faster. But her high heels were way too high and way too pointy. She stumbled and almost fell. She managed to catch herself, but the kite string went slack. The pink and purple kite plummeted toward the ground.

"Watch out!" Roxy shouted. She began sprinting in Miley's direction. "Kite gone wild! Kite gone wild!"

Startled, Miley turned just in time to see

the kite diving toward her head! She ducked, trying to avoid it, and the kite swooped past, trailing its string over her right shoulder.

Before Miley could breathe a sigh of relief, however, another gust of wind blew the kite back in the opposite direction! It was almost as if the kite was chasing her down!

She darted away again, but the kite had looped around so that the string was now tied around her shoulders. She tried to untangle herself, but somehow the kite—which now seemed to have a mind of its own, and an evil one at that—wrapped around her again.

By the time Roxy reached her, Miley was red-faced, panting, and completely tied up with the kite string.

"How in heaven's name did you get yourself in this mess?" Roxy asked.

"I was attacked by a kite," Miley said mournfully. "And the kite won."

 *Chapter Four*

Oh, yes, I have a clipper ship,
She's called the Henry Clay,
She sails away at break of day.
                    —"We're All Bound to Go"

Fortunately, by the afternoon Miley felt much happier. She and Roxy had stopped at a cute little restaurant, where she ate an omelet with french fries for lunch. Afterward, they stopped at an ice-cream shop, where Miley got a chocolate-mint double-scoop cone, which more than made up for the chocolate-vanilla–swirl cone that had landed on the pavement earlier.

Now, Miley was strolling along in the

sunshine in comfortable sneakers, wig-free, eating her ice cream and headed for the water-front where the ship she had noticed earlier was now docked.

As she and Roxy got closer to the water and the ship, they saw the boy Miley had noticed earlier polishing a brass rail.

"I wonder what his name is?" Miley said idly, not really expecting an answer.

But then, as if in answer to her question, a gruff voice called out, "Sam, you want to go get us some lunch?"

"His name is Sam," Miley whispered, delighted with this information. She tossed the last of her ice-cream cone in a nearby trash can. She turned to Roxy. "How does my hair look? Is my mascara smeared? Do I have ice cream on my face?"

"Calm down, girl," Roxy said. "You look cute as a button."

Sam shouted back, "Aye, aye, Captain Dan. How about a sandwich from Patty's?"

An older man emerged on the deck. He was burly and balding, dressed in weather-beaten shorts and a faded T-shirt. "That sure would hit the spot," he said. "Pastrami on rye for me. Ask Patty for an extra pickle, would ya?"

As Sam jumped down to the dock, Captain Dan grabbed a line and began hoisting a sail with brisk efficiency, his muscles rippling.

"Mm-mm-mm," Roxy murmured, raising an eyebrow.

"Oh, no, Roxy," Miley said, pretending to sound stern. "I see what you're looking at."

Roxy jumped guiltily. "Like you said, that's one *fiiiine*-looking ship."

"Uh-huh." Miley nodded solemnly.

"Chock-full of history," Roxy said.

"Right." Miley gave her a wink.

"You know how much I love history," Roxy added.

Miley would have continued teasing Roxy, but she could see Sam walking toward them. Hurriedly, she asked, "Roxy, can you maybe make yourself scarce for a few minutes?"

Roxy turned to see what had caught Miley's attention. "Oh, I see," she said dryly. "You want me to vanish—"

"Well, yeah . . ." Miley bit her lip. Sam was getting closer.

"You want me to vamoose."

"If you don't mind," Miley said, trying to resist the urge to make shooing motions.

"In fact, you want me to go"—Roxy waved her hands in the air as if performing a magic trick—"all invisible on you!"

"*Please.*" Miley gave her a gentle push in the direction of the ship. "Why don't you go talk to that nice Captain Dan? He could probably tell you all about sails and ropes and . . . I don't know, nautical things."

Roxy hesitated. "Well, I never want to stand in the way of young love."

"Thank you!" Miley said.

"But remember—Roxy's always got her eyes on you." She leaned in so that her nose was almost touching Miley's. "See these babies?" She pointed to her eyes. "Not even blinking."

"Fine, I got it; you'd win a staring contest with a totem pole," Miley said. "Now, go!"

Chuckling under her breath, Roxy sauntered toward the gangplank just as Sam reached Miley.

"Hi," Miley said, giving him a smiling glance. "Nice boat."

He met her eyes for a nanosecond, then looked away. "Thanks," he muttered.

Huh, Miley thought, puzzled by this cool response. Well, maybe he's the strong, silent type . . . or maybe he just needs a little help getting the conversation going.

"My name's Miley," she said brightly. "Miley Stewart."

He stared at the ground.

Okay, maybe he needs a *lot* of help. "And your name is . . . ?"

"Sam!" Captain Dan yelled from the ship. "Pastrami! Pickles! Patty's!"

Sam saluted the captain. "My name's Sam

Bliss," he said quickly. "But I can't talk. Gotta go. Sorry."

He didn't sound sorry at all, Miley thought crossly. More like relieved.

"No problem." Miley said as casually as she could. "Maybe I'll see you around."

He nodded, and now the look of utter relief was even more obvious.

Fine, Miley thought. There are plenty of other fish in the sea. . . .

But then she suddenly found herself walking alongside him. He glanced over at her, an odd expression on his face.

"Do you mind if I walk with you?" she asked cheerfully. "I've heard Patty's sandwiches are the best on the island." She pushed the memory of the omelet, french fries, and ice-cream cone she had just eaten to the back of her mind. "And I'm starving," she added.

He shrugged. "Sure."

As they walked along, Miley tried to think of ways to get Sam to talk. Fortunately, she knew a lot about being interviewed. Now it was time to turn the tables. . . .

By the time Miley and Sam were on their way back to the ship, she had acquired a few—but just a few—facts about Sam. Still, she congratulated herself for now knowing the following:

Sam began sailing when he was seven.

He was now seventeen.

He owned a small sailboat.

And he worked for Captain Dan during the summer.

Those few pieces of hard-won information wouldn't be enough for two paragraphs in a magazine article, Miley thought with exasperation. Feeling a new respect for interviewers, she tried again. "So, what exactly do you do for Captain Dan?" she asked, trying to make her voice warm and encouraging.

"Anything he asks me to," Sam said. Then he lapsed back into silence.

Miley gritted her teeth and made an effort to sound pleasant. "I see," she said. "So, do you run tourist excursions?"

"Yeah," he said.

Miley grinned eagerly and waited for him to go on. But he didn't. Miley sighed. Here she was, showing an interest in what he was interested in, the way all the teen magazines suggested, and yet she was getting nowhere. And they were almost back to the boat. In a few minutes, their conversation—what there was of it—would be over. If only she had more time to spend with him . . .

She took a deep breath. Time to take a chance here, she told herself. If only her palms weren't sweating and her stomach didn't feel like ice . . .

Hey, come on, she reminded herself. You've got nerve, right?

She took a deep breath and blurted out, "So, maybe we could hang out. When you're in port, that is. If you're not too busy, I mean . . ."

Her voice trailed off. Lame, lame, lame!

"But you probably are," she added hastily. "Busy, I mean. I'm sure you have to spend a lot of time polishing the ship and talking to tourists and stuff like that—"

He shrugged. "Not really."

Miley walked for three steps in silence as she tried to figure out what that meant. Was he saying he wasn't really busy so he would like to hang out? Or was he saying that she had his duties all wrong? Or was he saying . . .

She risked a quick glance at Sam. His face looked blank, but the tips of his ears had turned bright red.

This is terrible! Miley thought. How could she possibly get out of this horrible, awkward, embarrassing situation. . . .

"Hey, Miley!" Roxy was grinning and waving at her cheerfully. Standing next to her was Captain Dan.

"Um . . . hey." Miley was astonished. Roxy had a look on her face that Miley had never seen before. She looked practically . . . giddy.

Captain Dan took the paper bag with his lunch in it from Sam. "I was beginning to think you'd been lost at sea," he said. He tilted his baseball cap back and smiled at Miley. "I'm Dan McIntyre, but everybody calls me Captain Dan."

"Hi," Miley said, shaking his hand. "Roxy, this is Sam Bliss. Sam, this is Roxy, my body— um, my buddy. Yeah, that's who she is. My buddy."

"Hi." Sam nodded at Roxy.

But Roxy was hardly looking at Sam. Instead, she was beaming at Captain Dan.

"Dan's been the captain of this ship for twenty-two years," Roxy told Miley. "He was just telling me all about these wonderful dolphin-watching cruises he takes people on. I'd love to see dolphins, wouldn't you, Miley? In fact, I've *always* wanted to see dolphins."

Miley gave her an incredulous look. The only dolphins she'd ever heard Roxy talk about were the Miami Dolphins—and that was only to abuse them for upsetting her favorite team, the New England Patriots.

The captain smiled into Roxy's eyes. "Well, I don't guarantee you'll see them, of course. Dolphins play by their own rules, you know."

"Tell me about it." Roxy's face darkened slightly.

Captain Dan looked slightly confused by this reaction, but he added, "Even if we don't see dolphins, it's still a nice day on the water. Just let me know if you'd like to go out some time."

"That's a deal," Roxy said.

As this conversation went on, Miley alternated between feeling amused at Roxy's sudden gift for flirting and depressed at the difference between her bodyguard's budding romance and her own prospects for summer fun.

Sam, she couldn't help but notice, was shifting from foot to foot. He looked as if he couldn't wait to get away from them. Sure enough, he took full advantage of a lull in the conversation to say, "Hey, Cap, didn't you want me to bring that box on board? I can do that right now, if you want."

"Right." Captain Dan scratched his head as he studied a small wooden crate at the end of the gangplank. "Thing is, Joe borrowed my handcart—"

"Oh, I could handle that bad boy," Roxy said. "You know, I bench three hundred."

"No, really," Captain Dan said, looking rather alarmed. "You don't have to—"

"No problem." Roxy picked up the box and hefted it in the air a few times. Then she said cheerfully, "Light as a feather. Now just tell me where you want it."

Captain Dan blinked, his mouth agape. "Um, just on the deck," he stammered. "Thanks."

Roxy nodded, then walked up the gangplank, put the box down, and returned. She wasn't even breathing hard.

"See?" she said. "Easy as pie."

"Well." Captain Dan seemed to be at a loss for words. "If you ever need a job, I'd hire you for my crew any day."

"Thanks. I'll keep that in mind." Roxy smiled into his eyes for a long moment. Then a clock from a nearby church chimed, breaking the spell. "I guess we'd better go," she said, glancing at Miley. "We've got, um, that thing we gotta do, right, Miley?"

Miley nodded glumly. In the middle of the photo shoot, the *Entertainment Insider* editors had e-mailed interview questions for Hannah Montana to Jeremy. Miley had agreed to e-mail her answers back to them before the end of the day. At the time, it hadn't seemed like a big deal, but now . . .

Miley cast an imploring glance at Roxy, hoping her bodyguard would realize that it would make much more sense for Miley to conduct her own interview . . . with Sam. Surely, if she worked a little harder, she could get him to talk. . . .

But Roxy ignored her look, put a firm hand on Miley's arm, and began saying good-bye.

"It was real nice meeting both of you," Roxy said.

"Same here," Captain Dan said warmly.

As they left, a ray of sunshine shot through a cloud and picked out the ship's name, which was painted on the back in gold. Miley's eyes widened. The ship was called *Trueheart*.

"Look, Roxy," Miley said, pointing to the ship's stern. "What a romantic name." She glanced slyly at Roxy. "It's like a sign, don't you think?"

"You and your signs," Roxy scoffed.

But Miley noticed that Roxy turned to look at the ship one last time as they walked away.

Chapter Five

We'll rant and we'll roar like true Yankee
*   whalermen,*
We'll rant and we'll roar on deck and below
Until we sight Gayhead off Old Martha's
*   Vineyard,*
And straight up the Channel to New Bedford
*   we'll go.*

*   —"Yankee Whalerman"*

Miley wasn't the only one with drama in her life. The very first night of Lilly and Oliver's stay, Mrs. Kilpatrick prepared a very special dinner for them.

But there was something about the way her great-aunt had said "very special" that made

Lilly uneasy. Perhaps it was because she seemed to be enjoying a private joke, one that Lilly and Oliver would, perhaps, not find very funny.

Oh, I'm just tired from the trip, she told herself. It's making me imagine things. Great-aunt Agatha isn't really *that* strange. . . .

But now, as she and Oliver sat down on opposite sides of a heavy-oak dining table, ready to be served that "very special" dinner, Lilly wasn't so sure. The dining room was a cavernous space with dark red walls. The windows were draped with dusty velvet curtains; several strange statues were set in the corners; and, even in the dim light, Lilly could see cobwebs hanging from the ceiling. The room was lit with a dozen flickering candles, which cast strange shadows and made even Oliver's friendly face look distorted and unreal.

Mrs. Kilpatrick came in from the kitchen, carrying a platter of roast chicken. Bowls of mashed potatoes and green beans were already on the table. "Here we go!" she said. "Doesn't this smell delicious?"

Oliver's eyes brightened. "It smells *fantastic*," he said, sniffing the air. "You used herbs on the chicken, didn't you? In fact . . . is that rosemary I smell? And perhaps a touch of thyme?"

Lilly smirked a bit at that. Oliver had recently become addicted to TV cooking shows and was constantly trying to show off his knowledge.

Mrs. Kilpatrick gave him a sly smile and held the platter out so that he could pick up a piece of chicken with a pair of heavy silver tongs. "Thank you, Oliver," she said. "You have an excellent olfactory sense. I used the very same recipe my character Chantal used to poison her husband in *Slay It with Spices.* Rosemary does an excellent job of masking the scent of arsenic, you know."

Oliver lost his grip on the tongs. The chicken leg went flying across the room, followed closely by a black streak of fur.

"Marlowe!" Mrs. Kilpatrick said sharply as the cat picked up the chicken leg with its teeth. *"Loco ut down!"*

Marlowe gave her a baleful stare, but finally, after several seconds, dropped the chicken leg. He stalked toward the kitchen, his tail held high. When he reached the door, he turned his head, gave her a long look and meowed loudly.

"Same to you," Mrs. Kilpatrick replied with a chuckle.

Marlowe seemed to toss his head before sauntering out of the room, as if he'd planned to leave all along.

"Wh-what did you just say to him?" Oliver asked nervously.

Mrs. Kilpatrick laughed. "I just said, 'put that down!' in Latin," she explained. "It's the only language Marlowe really responds to. When I try French, he does the opposite of what he's told; when I use Dutch, he goes to sleep; and English . . . well, he completely ignores me if I speak English."

Lilly gave the older woman a sharp look. Was she kidding, or did she really think her cat understood her? And, if so, did she really think he knew *four* languages?

Her great-aunt put the platter down in the middle of the table. "I'll just throw that chicken leg away," she said. "You two go ahead and serve yourselves."

She picked up the dusty chicken and swept out of the room. As soon as she was gone, Oliver leaned across the table and hissed to Lilly, "She knows how to mask the scent of arsenic! She speaks Latin to her cat! *And* she thinks the cat understands her! Now do you see why I'm worried?"

"Shh!" Lilly hissed. "That's called being eccentric, Oliver. You're freaking out over nothing."

"She made us the same chicken that Chantal served in *Slay It with Spices*," Oliver reminded Lilly. "Have you ever read that book?"

"No," Lilly said. "And I don't want to

hear anything about it that will keep me from eating this chicken! I'm starving!"

At that moment, Mrs. Kilpatrick came back into the room and sat down at the head of the table. "So, tonight, in addition to *chicken à la Chantal*, we have mashed potatoes with sour cream—"

"Yum," Lilly said, taking a big scoop. "That sounds great."

But Oliver looked ill. "Are those, by any chance, the same mashed potatoes that Freddy Richardson used to knock off his business partner in *Truth or Die*?"

Mrs. Kilpatrick gave him a glinting smile as she handed him the gravy boat. "You know my work," Mrs. Kilpatrick purred. "Dear, dear boy."

She delicately transferred a chicken breast from the platter to her own plate. "You're quite right, Oliver. In fact, the green beans are the only dish that doesn't have a connection to my novels," Lilly's great-aunt added cheerfully, apparently not noticing her guests' sudden lack of appetite. "I realized as I was planning my menu that I've never used poisoned vegetables in any of my novels. Perhaps that's a good thing; after all, why give people even more reason not to eat them? On the other hand—"

She got a distracted look on her face as she stared at the green bean she had just speared with her fork. "Perhaps this is an opportunity?" she murmured to herself. "Readers would never expect a simple side dish to be an instrument of death. . . . Brussels sprouts might be good. I could have a character who has a special fondness for them . . . no one else will touch them, of course, so the murderer could be sure that only his intended victim would die. . . . Hmmm, yes, that could work. . . ."

Oliver glumly took an extra helping of green beans. His mother, he thought, would be astonished. "It's good to know there's something on this table that hasn't been used to kill somebody," he said.

Mrs. Kilpatrick's eyes twinkled. "Don't worry, I don't make a habit of killing my guests at their very first dinner," she told him.

Lilly watched as Oliver, looking somewhat reassured, took a cautious bite of mashed potatoes. She held her breath as he chewed and swallowed. She counted to ten . . . and then, seeing that he was still sitting upright and breathing, she dared to take a bite herself.

She was glad she did. The potatoes were creamy, with just a hint of tanginess. She relaxed a little and began enjoying her meal.

Great-aunt Agatha might be a little odd, Lilly thought, and her taste in dining-room decoration was unnerving, to say the least. But Lilly's own mother sang ABBA songs while she cooked dinner and insisted on displaying all of Lilly's school photos on their dining-room sideboard, which was just as horrifying in its own way.

Lilly smiled to herself, pleased at how she

had been able to use logic to make the case that her great-aunt was just slightly dotty and totally harmless. . . .

And that's when she tuned back in to the conversation Oliver and Mrs. Kilpatrick were having.

"So, here's what I was wondering when I was reading *Frozen with Fear*," Oliver said, an intense look in his eyes. "In that book, Poppy La Tour stabs Ralph Whitmore with an icicle, which melts before the police arrive. A perfect plan!"

"Almost perfect," Mrs. Kilpatrick reminded him with a smile. "My books always end with the killer brought to justice."

"Okay," Oliver said. "But how did that work at all? I mean, in real life, the icicle would break, wouldn't it?"

"Actually, no," Mrs. Kilpatrick answered, looking slightly smug. "But that's a very good question, and one I wondered about myself. I decided that I had to do my own experiment to see whether that plot twist would work—you see, I always research my books quite thoroughly. For *Frozen with Fear*, I actually created icicles in my freezer that were quite long and sharp—"

"And then you *stabbed* people with them?" Oliver asked, his voice suddenly turning into a squeak.

"Well, no," she admitted. "True, that would have been the very best way to prove my hypothesis, but I decided that would be going a bit too far. So I bought a turkey at the supermarket and stabbed it instead. Several times, in fact."

"You stabbed a turkey," Oliver repeated slowly.

"Thawed, naturally," she said, nodding. "It was surprisingly difficult. I was panting by the time I was done and had to pour myself a cup of restorative tea afterward. Which is, of course, exactly what Poppy did!"

Lilly carefully avoided meeting Oliver's

eyes. Even she was feeling a little uneasy about the way this conversation was going, which meant, she knew, that he was probably on the verge of full-on panic.

"But enough!" Mrs. Kilpatrick said briskly. "I could talk about how I research my books for hours, which I'm sure you would both find quite boring. So now I'd like to go over a few of my house rules. There aren't many, and they're very simple to follow, I assure you."

Lilly and Oliver waited.

"I'll give you a house key so you can go biking or to the beach whenever you want," she said. "Please make sure you lock the door if you leave and I'm not here."

They nodded. That made sense.

"Always close the front gate behind you, so Marlowe can't get out," she went on. "He thinks he has an excellent sense of direction, but I can assure you he's quite wrong about that. I warn you, you can't believe a word he says. That cat could get lost in the back garden.

"And finally, the most important rule of all." Mrs. Kilpatrick paused and leaned forward, her eyes glinting with seriousness. "You may explore the house all you want, with one exception." She lowered her voice, fixed her stern gaze on their faces, and said in a fierce whisper, "You must never go in the attic." She paused for a second, then repeated the word, *"Never!"*

Both Lilly and Oliver jumped. As if realizing that she had unnerved them, Mrs. Kilpatrick relaxed slightly and dabbed at her lips with her napkin. "I don't wish to be inhospitable, but I use the attic to store certain . . . objects that are quite dear to me. I would hate for anything to happen to them. I'm sure you understand."

They gulped.

"We understand," Lilly said in a small voice. "Don't worry."

Her great-aunt Agatha smiled and sat back in her chair. "Excellent!" she said. "I knew I could count on your good sense. Now . . . who would like dessert?"

After the dishes had been washed and Great-aunt Agatha had gone to bed, Lilly crept across the hallway from her bedroom to Oliver's and carefully opened his door. When she peeked inside, she saw that he was sitting up in bed, reading one of Mrs. Kilpatrick's mysteries. She took a step, and the floorboards creaked under her foot.

Oliver screamed.

"*Shh!*" Lilly hissed as she quickly shut the door behind her. "What's wrong with you?"

"What's *wrong* with me? What's wrong with *me*?" Oliver stared at her. "Oh, I don't know, Lilly. I guess I'm a little on edge. Seeing as how we're trapped in a creepy mansion in the middle of nowhere with a maniac!"

"Oliver, you always exaggerate," Lilly said.

He grabbed the pile of books on his bedside table and started holding up one after the other in front of Lilly's face. "Do I, Lilly?" he asked. "Do I, really? Take a look at these titles: *Arsenic in the Aspic. A Soupçon of Cyanide. Murder by Marmalade. Death Goes to Brunch.* And what about all that talk at dinner about stabbing defenseless turkeys with icicles? Your great-aunt is seriously spooky."

"Oh, come on, she's not that bad," Lilly protested, but she knew she didn't sound very convincing.

"She talks to her cat in Latin, and she thinks he talks back!" Oliver said. "How well does your mother know her, anyway?"

Lilly bit her lip. "Well, here's the thing . . ." she began.

Oliver looked at her. "Yeah?"

Lilly gave him a forced smile. "Well, my mom hasn't actually seen Great-aunt Agatha for fifteen years."

"Just as I thought," Oliver said darkly. "And since the last time she saw her, your great-aunt has gone *craaaazy!*"

Lilly looked uncomfortable. "Maybe not. Mom said that Great-aunt Agatha was always eccentric—"

"Eccentric? Eccentric is someone who collects potatoes that look like world leaders!" Oliver said. "Not someone who keeps a mummy in the living room!"

"Oh, come on, Oliver, that's a papier-mâché sculpture she made in a workshop in South America," Lilly said. Though she had to admit that at first glance the figure had startled her, with its gruesome features and odd, menacing posture. But still . . . "It's not a mummy, it's *art*."

"*And* there's something terrible hidden in the attic," Oliver finished in a whisper.

Lilly jumped. "Stop it, Oliver. You're creeping me out!"

"*I'm* creeping *you* out?" he cried. "It's your great-aunt who's stashed a body just two floors above us."

"Who said the locked room has a body in

it?" Lilly said, trying to cling to a shred of logic. "She said the room 'holds items of great importance' to her. Maybe she found a buried treasure on the beach. You know, a pirate's trunk filled with gold doubloons!"

"She would have put them in a bank," Oliver argued.

"Maybe the attic is where she keeps mementos from her childhood."

"Then why wouldn't she let us see them?" Oliver asked her. "Most old people love to talk about the good ole days when they were young."

"Well, okay, then maybe—"

"Face it, Lilly," Oliver interrupted. "There is something suspicious about your great-aunt Agatha. But don't worry." He picked up another book from his pile. "I have a feeling that every clue we need is hidden in her books. And if I keep reading, I'll find out what they are."

Chapter Six

I've done with the toils of the seas,
Ye sailors, I'm bound to my love.
  —"Come, Loose Every Sail to the Breeze"

"Okay, Hannah, let's see a big smile!" Chad called out. "It's a beautiful, sunny day, you're having fun on the beach, you don't have a care in the world. . . . That's right, great. You're looking wonderful, keep it up—"

All right, Miley thought as she smiled at the camera and danced across the sand, stopping occasionally to smile over her shoulder or turn a cartwheel. This is more like what a photo shoot should be! Lighthearted, happy, and, most important, accident-free.

They had arrived at the beach at dawn in order to set up and be ready for the early-morning light. Now, two hours later, she hadn't tripped, fallen on her face in the sand, or spilled any food items on her outfit.

Out of the corner of her eye, she could see Roxy standing with her arms folded and her face serious, scanning the small crowd that had gathered to watch, ready to leap into action at the first sign that a fan might try to get too close. A short distance away, Jeremy walked up to Chad to discuss how the shoot was going. Josie and Sabrina, clearly bored when they weren't being called upon to powder Hannah's nose or fix her outfit between shots, were sitting on towels, working on their tans.

"I think that's enough of this setup," Chad said. "Hannah, why don't you take a break while I change lenses?"

"Sure thing," Miley said. She jogged over to

Roxy, who had a bottle of water ready to hand her. Miley took a swig and grinned at her bodyguard. "I think I've reversed the curse," she said. "The curse of klutziness, that is."

"Uh-huh." Roxy sounded unconvinced. "Well, don't get your hopes up, baby."

"Hey, come on!" Miley said. "I can dream, can't I?"

"Okay, Hannah, we're ready," Chad yelled.

Miley took a last sip of water and ran back to the photographer. "What do you want me to do now?"

He looked out at the waves and pursed his lips thoughtfully. "We've got a lot of good shots of you on the beach," he said. "Why don't you wade out into the water, just up to your knees? I like the idea of you against the blue water and the blue sky. Could be a very nice photo."

"Sure," Miley said, slipping off her sandals. As she stepped into the water, she felt the tug and pull of the waves against her legs. A seagull gave a raucous cry as it flew overhead. In the distance, she could hear the shouts from a spirited beach-volleyball game.

Sometimes, she thought, it was good to remember what a great job she had. Here she was, working . . . but working meant standing on the beach on a glorious summer day. She smiled as she took a few more steps, then turned to face Chad.

"Is this far enough?" she yelled.

He gave her a thumbs-up. "Great," he yelled back. "Now, smile. Toss your head. That's it, fantastic. Your hair looks great. . . ."

Miley turned this way and that, put her hands on her hips, and looked over her shoulder to wink at the camera. This was fun . . . and it was helping her forget yesterday's disastrous photo shoot. These shots were sure to be great, she thought . . .

. . . just as a wall of cold water came crashing down on her and knocked her over! A tall wave had caught her completely off guard.

"Stupid wave," she muttered as, coughing and blinking, she tried to struggle to her feet.

Then she heard Roxy yelling, "Don't move, Hannah, I'll save you!"

Before Miley could yell back that she didn't need saving—after all, the water around her was only a couple of feet deep—Roxy reached her.

"Roxy, I'm fine, really—" Miley started to say.

But before she'd even finished her sentence, Roxy grabbed Miley by the shoulders and pushed her under the water!

After a few shocked seconds, Miley started to twist around, trying to get free. Then, just as she thought her lungs would burst, Roxy pulled her out of the water.

"What . . . are . . . you . . . doing?" Miley gasped in a strangled voice.

Roxy wrapped her arms around Miley, shielding her from the people on the beach. "Are you okay?" she asked.

"Yes," Miley said, taking deep breaths. "No thanks to you! Didn't they teach you right in bodyguard school? You're supposed to *save* people, not *kill* them!"

"Is that so?" Roxy snapped. "Well, your daddy gave me another little job, namely keeping your secret identity a *secret*."

Miley blinked stinging seawater out of her eyes, then glared up at her. "And how does drowning me fit in with that part of your job description?"

"Take a look," Roxy said, holding up a wet, stringy, blond mess. "That wave knocked off your Hannah hair. I just managed to grab this before it got swept out to sea."

"Oh." Miley smiled weakly. "Thanks. And . . . sorry for yelling."

"No problem. Hold still," Roxy said. She plopped the limp wig on Miley's head, then squinted at her. "Well, you look like a drowned rat, but at least you look like one named Hannah instead of one named Miley."

"And I was just thinking how well today's photo shoot was going," Miley said mournfully, making her way back to the beach.

"Well, that was your big mistake," Roxy told her. "You jinxed yourself. Never think things are going fine. That's a bodyguard's number-one rule."

"I'll try to remember that," Miley said. As she walked across the sand, she noticed that Chad had his camera out and was still taking pictures.

"Hey!" she said, holding her hands in front of her face. "You don't want pictures of me looking like this."

He lowered his camera and blinked at her. "I don't?"

"No!" she almost yelled. "I mean, look at me!"

"Oh, don't worry, Hannah," Chad said. "Sure, you look a little bedraggled right now, but we'll make sure you look fantastic in the magazine. Won't we, Jeremy?"

The art director looked doubtful, but he nodded. "We've done more with less," he said with a heavy sigh. "Why don't you take the rest of the afternoon off to . . . freshen up."

"I'd better get Hannah back to her room so she can change," Roxy said, before Miley could snap back an answer.

"Of course," Jeremy said. "Let me get you a car—"

"Oh, don't bother," Miley said. "I like walking. And the air will dry me off."

And the sooner I get out of here and get back to looking like Miley Stewart, the better, she thought to herself.

As they walked back to the Bumblebee Inn, Miley began to feel more cheerful. True, the day had ended up being a bit of a bust. But now she had the whole afternoon free . . . and she knew exactly how she wanted to spend it.

"Once we get cleaned up, maybe we should get a bite of lunch," Miley said to Roxy, as offhandedly as possible. "Maybe we should go back to that cute little sandwich place. Maybe we should stroll around for a while after lunch—"

"And maybe you should quit trying to pull the wool over Roxy's eyes," her bodyguard said, giving her a no-nonsense look. "I know exactly what you're trying to do, you're trying to run into that boy again, that—"

"Sam!" a voice yelled from behind them, making them both jump. Then a boy whizzed past them on a skateboard, still yelling, "Hey, where are you heading? You want to go surfing today?"

Miley turned her head to see Sam walking down the street—right toward them!

"It's him!" she hissed to Roxy.

Miley watched as Sam stopped to chat with his skateboarding friend. He was just a few feet away; fortunately, his back was to Miley and Roxy, so he hadn't seen them . . . yet. But he could turn around at any minute—and not only that, he was standing right in front of the Bumblebee Inn. There was no way Miley could enter without him spotting her.

"He can't see me like this!" Miley cried, ducking behind the nearest tree. "I look like a cat that got dragged through a hedge backward."

Roxy gave her a fleeting glance. "Yep," she said. "And then fell in a mud puddle."

"Roxy!" she wailed. "You have to help me out here."

"Don't worry, honey, no one's going to see you." Roxy pressed her lips together and stared intently across the street. "We just got to take evasive action and determine an alternate form of access."

"Secret agent, say what?" Miley asked.

"We need to figure out a different way to get you into your room," Roxy translated. She squinted thoughtfully over at the hotel entrance. After a few moments, she nodded. "Okay, I got it." She winked at Miley. "And

I don't mean nerve, either."

"Ha-ha, very funny." Miley was starting to shiver, despite it being a warm summer day. "I hope you meant you got an idea on how to deal with this situation."

"Oh, I do," Roxy said. "I do, indeed. Now, here's the plan. I'll walk over there and chat with the boys. That will distract them long enough for you to go back the way we came, cross at the far corner, and sneak down the alley that runs behind the inn. I'll meet you in ten minutes, and we'll go from there."

"Okay, but . . ." Miley began.

Roxy snapped her fingers in Miley's face. "But me—no buts, girl!" she said. "Just make sure you get *your* butt across the street lickety-split. I can only provide fascinating conversation for so long, you know."

Miley hugged the brick wall of the nearby drugstore. She had made it as far as the corner. Now she just had to dash across the street and run up the alley without Sam seeing her.

She stared at the asphalt that lay in between her and sanctuary. That's a skinny little excuse for a road, she thought, trying to encourage herself. Shoot, if that were a creek back in Tennessee, you'd probably try to jump it.

Of course, leaping over a creek implied a certain carefree spirit, something she definitely wasn't feeling right now.

Slowly she peeked around the corner of the building. She could see Roxy and Sam. The skateboarding boy seemed to have taken off, and Sam was nodding and laughing at something Roxy had said.

For a moment, Miley enjoyed just standing there and watching him from afar. The day before she hadn't noticed how wavy his hair was or how his golden tan seemed to glow. . . .

Then she caught herself. She was forgetting her mission.

"Focus, Miley," she whispered to herself.

One more glance down the street told her

that Roxy had managed to get Sam to move so that his back was to Miley. She took a deep breath and sprinted across the street, past the office building on the opposite corner and down the alley. She reached the back of the inn panting, but very proud.

Miley paused for a moment to take a look around. Flower beds filled with white, pink, and purple flowers ran along a white fence around the edge of the inn's backyard. An enormous lilac bush stood in one corner of the yard, while an oak tree spread its branches over the lawn. Miley wiggled her toes in the cool green grass and thought longingly of how nice it would be to just stretch out and daydream the afternoon away. . . .

But just then, she heard voices. Roxy and Sam were walking down the narrow sidewalk that ran along the side of the inn, and they were coming closer by the second.

"So, Sam, you're here to help with the baking," Roxy said.

She was talking in an unnaturally loud voice. Miley knew what that meant. It was a warning! She was about to be discovered! Her heart racing, she looked around frantically for a hiding place. That's when she saw the lilac bush. She quickly pushed her way through its branches and then stood as still as possible.

"Well, my aunt is the inn's cook and the owner of the Bayside Baker, so she has a lot of baking to do," Sam replied. "And I don't mind helping out on cookie-baking night, since I get to eat any cookies that don't pass my aunt's inspection."

As Sam was saying that, he and Roxy reached the backyard. From inside the lilac bush, Miley could see her bodyguard scan the area, then look relieved to find that Miley wasn't there.

"Well, I'd better get to work," Sam said. "Um . . . say hi to Miley for me."

"I'll be sure to do that," Roxy said. "And please tell Captain Dan hi for me!"

Inside her green and leafy hiding place, Miley smiled. Sam remembered her name! And he said to say hello!

Sam opened the back door and went into the inn's kitchen. As the door closed behind him, the faint smell of chocolate chip cookies, still warm from the oven, wafted through the air.

"Miley!" Roxy whispered. "Where are you?"

Miley rustled the lilac branches in reply. Roxy walked over, casting a glance or two over her shoulder to make sure she wasn't being watched from inside the kitchen.

"Is that you?" Roxy hissed.

"No, it's the Ghost of Lilacs Past!" Miley hissed back. "Of course it's me! This was the only place to hide."

"That was fast thinking," Roxy said.

"So I heard Sam ask you to say hello to me!" Miley went on, excited. "Were you guys talking about me earlier? What did he say? Did he remember me, or did you have to remind him about who I was? Did he sound like he liked me? Did he seem—"

"Honey, as much as I'd like to debrief you on our conversation, we've got more important things to worry about," Roxy snapped. "Like making sure that Sam keeps thinking you're Miley. Which means getting you back to your room without him seeing you."

"Oh. Right." Miley settled back down.

"I thought we'd go in the back, but I guess that's out," Roxy said.

Through the window, Miley could see Sam's aunt hand him an apron. Several large mixing bowls and a dozen cookie sheets were spread out on the kitchen table. Clearly, cookie-baking night could go on for some time.

"Why don't we just go in through the front door, now that Sam's in the kitchen?" Miley asked.

"Uh-uh, honey, you never know when he might decide to go out that way," Roxy said. "Anyway, I think I see a solution to our problem right over there."

She pointed to the side of the house. Miley peered through the leaves.

"What?" she asked. "I don't see anything but those roses climbing up the wall. . . ."

"Climbing up a *lattice*," Roxy corrected her. "Which we can also climb."

Instantly, a flashback to a certain disastrous gym class appeared in Miley's mind. "Um, I'm actually not that good at wall-climbing," she began.

"Don't worry, Roxy'll be right behind you," her bodyguard said. "And I can give you a pretty big push if necessary."

"Great," Miley said, staring glumly at the roses. "This should be fun."

A short time later, Miley managed to get her head and shoulders inside her bedroom window. Her face was sweaty, her wig had fallen forward over her face, and her arms and legs were covered with scratches from the roses' thorns.

She paused, breathing hard and trying to summon up the strength to actually get the rest of her body through the window and into the sanctuary of her room.

She fixed her gaze on the bathroom door and thought encouraging thoughts about taking a nice, long, hot shower and shampooing her hair, now stiff with dried seawater. . . .

Then something shoved her from behind. "Hey!" She turned her head to glare down at Roxy, who was clinging to the lattice right beneath her. "I just needed to take a break for a second," she complained.

"This lattice is the thing that's about to *break* if you don't get a move on," Roxy said. "It's built to handle roses, not people. Especially not a full-figured person like myself."

Miley heard the lattice creak ominously. "Okay, okay," she muttered.

She used her arms to pull herself forward, and with a little wiggling—and one last emphatic push from Roxy—she finally popped through and landed in a heap on the floor. Roxy followed minutes later, and they both crawled over to collapse on their beds.

Roxy stared at the ceiling, breathing hard. "I'm getting too old for this," she muttered.

"You and me both," Miley sighed. "And I'm *years* younger than you!"

Giggling, she dodged the pillow Roxy threw at her and darted into the bathroom.

"Dibs on the shower!"

 *Chapter Seven*

Blow the wind
South o'er the bonnie blue sea.
        —*"Blow the Wind Southerly"*

As Miley and Roxy walked down to the wharf later that evening, Miley begged for the tenth time, "Tell me again what Sam said about me!"

Roxy rolled her eyes. "Miley, I'm only going to go over this once more, because it's getting real tedious," she warned. "For the last time. He remembered me and said hello. Then I said hello. Then he said, 'Where's Miley?' Then I said, 'Oh, around here somewhere.' Then we started talking about sailing and cookies and other subjects that had *nothing to do with you*."

"He said, 'Where's Miley?'" Miley sighed. She smiled at Roxy. "That's my favorite part of the story."

But Roxy wasn't listening. She had paused in front of a store window and was frowning at her reflection. She reached up to tweak a curl back into place. "Are you sure I look all right? These ocean breezes are hard on Roxy's hairdo."

"For the last time," Miley said, copying Roxy's warning, "you look great. Now come on, it's getting late. . . ."

"Okay, o-*kay*," Roxy said as Miley dragged her away from the window. "I'm just trying to look stylin'."

Miley grinned.

"What?" Roxy asked.

"What, 'what'?" Miley said, doing her best to look puzzled.

"Why are you grinnin' to yourself like some kind of Cheshire Cat?" Roxy demanded.

Miley giggled. "It's just that you're so cute."

"Roxy is a lot of things," her bodyguard growled. "Cute ain't one of them."

"Oh, yes, yes, you are," Miley insisted. "Because you're nervous about seeing Captain Dan again. And you know what, I don't blame you." She leaned closer and, mimicking Roxy, said, "He's one *fiiiiine*-lookin' man."

Roxy gave her a suspicious glance. "I have a feeling you're making fun of me," she said.

"Who, me?" Miley tried to look the picture of innocence. Her gaze slipped past Roxy, and her face brightened. "Oh, look, there's the *Trueheart!*"

As they got closer, they saw that a half-dozen teenagers were on the ship, laughing and joking around. Then Sam appeared on deck, carrying a coil of rope.

"And, look, there's Sam!" Miley cried.

Then they reached the gangplank and

another person climbed out of the galley.

"And, oh, look," Miley said in dismay. "There's . . . Jackson."

At the sound of his name, Jackson turned in their direction and gave a jaunty salute. "Ahoy, there!" he yelled.

Miley saw Sam wave Jackson over and begin demonstrating how to tie a knot. Several other teens drifted over to watch, and even from a distance, Miley could see that Sam was chatting with all of them. She frowned. Where was the One-Word Answer that *she* had been introduced to?

Then she saw Sam laugh at something Jackson said, and she bit her lip, trying not to feel hurt. "What is *Jackson* doing on board the ship with Sam?" she asked Roxy.

"I don't know, but I have a feeling we're about to find out," Roxy said as Jackson bounded down the gangplank to greet them.

"Miley, Roxy, hi," he said. "So, guess who just earned a berth on the Good Ship *Trueheart*?"

"Someone who is not you?" Miley asked, her voice hopeful.

"Bzzzt!" Jackson imitated the sound of a game-show buzzer. "Wrong again! Oh, I'm sorry—game over!"

Miley opened her mouth to make a smart comeback, but then she saw Sam walking down the gangplank toward them.

"Hey, Sam," she said, feeling suddenly shy.

"Hey," Sam said, avoiding eye contact. "You guys know each other?"

Miley and Jackson heaved identical sighs. "My brother," Miley said in a put-upon voice, just as Jackson, in the exact same tone of voice, groaned, "My sister."

"Raise the mainsail," Captain Dan yelled from on the ship.

"Aye, aye, Captain," Sam yelled back.

As he ran lightly up the gangplank, Miley and Jackson squared off.

Jackson squinted suspiciously at Miley. "How do you know Sam?"

"I met him down here yesterday," she answered. "We walked to the sandwich shop, and we talked and . . . I think we had a moment."

Well, that wasn't a *complete* lie, Miley thought. At least, *she* had had a moment. Sam just needed a little time to catch up with her, that was all. . . .

"A moment?" Jackson scoffed. "A *moment*? Poor, dear, sweet Miley. Sam and I are like this." He held up two crossed fingers to demonstrate how close they were. "Sam and I have a bond. A dude bond. Which is a much bigger deal than a"—he made air quotes with his fingers—"'*moment.*'"

"Really." Miley raised an eyebrow. "So, how did you two meet and, you know, *bond*?"

Jackson shrugged. "I was walking around, looking at all the ships, and all of a sudden, I saw . . . that."

He pointed at the *Trueheart*. Now that Miley was closer, she saw that half the teens on deck were girls. All of them seemed to have golden suntans, gleaming white teeth, and long hair that they liked to toss in the breeze.

Jackson sighed happily at the sight. "I can't believe I ever thought that a vacation in Nantucket would be boring," he said. "What was I thinking?"

"Judging by your life so far, probably not much of anything," Miley snapped. "Get to the point!"

"Hmm?" Jackson was still gazing at the girls, who were now posing and taking pictures of each other with their camera phones. "Sorry, I forgot where we were. The point was—"

"Sam!" Miley said, trying not to raise her voice.

"Oh, yeah." Jackson reluctantly tore his gaze away from the ship and looked at Miley. "So, when he got off the ship, I asked him if he worked there, and we started talking. I told him how I always wanted to learn how to sail—"

"Say what?" Roxy had been listening in silence, but she couldn't keep quiet at that. "Boy, you used to get seasick watching those little aquarium fish at the dentist's office."

"Actually, it was just that one red fish that made me nauseous," Jackson said. "He always darted around like he'd had too much caffeine or something." He stifled a grimace as the memory flashed by. Then he leaned against the railing and crossed his arms, looking cocky. "But I've always been fascinated by the romance of the high seas, which is why it's so cool that Sam said I could help him out on the *Trueheart* and learn as I go."

Miley gasped. "You mean you're going to be on that ship all day . . . with Sam?" The unfairness of this made her head spin.

"Yep." Jackson grinned. "By the end of the week, I should be an old salt."

He turned to go up the gangplank, then promptly tripped over a coil of rope and fell down.

"Yeah," Miley said. "Or the object of a massive search-and-rescue operation."

"Now, Miley, it's a good thing for Jackson to make a friend," Roxy said. "After all, you've got Lilly and Oliver here, but Jackson's all alone—"

"Hey, Jackson, want to help with this?" Sam called, waving.

Miley watched as Jackson picked himself up and ran gleefully back up the gangplank. Then she turned to Roxy. "I know I have Lilly and Oliver," she cried. "But still! I can't believe Jackson is going to spend more time with Sam than I am! It's just so wrong in so many ways!"

"Is that a whine I hear in your voice?" Roxy asked sternly. "Because if it is. . . ." She let her voice trail off, but gave Miley a stern look. Miley knew Roxy hated whining. It was one of her pet peeves, along with talking behind people's backs and leaving wet towels on the bathroom floor. And it was no use to claim that you weren't whining if Roxy said you were. As she said, she was Judge Roxy, and she ruled the Court of No Complaints with an iron hand. The last time she had found Miley guilty of whining, Miley had ended up spending an entire Saturday afternoon scrubbing bathroom grout with a toothbrush.

"No!" Miley said quickly. "I'm just saying—"

But she didn't get to complete her sentence because, at that moment, Lilly and Oliver, smiling and sunburned, came running down the pier.

"Hey, Miley!" Lilly said.

"How did you know where to find us?" Oliver asked.

Miley shook her head, confused. "I didn't," she said. "I wasn't even looking for you. Why are you here?"

"Hey, have you seen our ship?" Oliver asked. "The teacher is this really cool guy named Captain Dan—"

"He's going to take us out on the water every day," Lilly said.

Oliver added, "And maybe even let us take the wheel sometimes—"

"It's not going to be like summer school at all!" Lilly finished, her eyes sparkling.

Miley's mouth dropped open. "You mean that"—she pointed at the *Trueheart*—"is the ship where your class is being held?"

"Yep," Oliver said.

"Pretty cool, huh?" Lilly added.

"Oh, yeah, it's pretty cool, all right," Miley said flatly. She honestly couldn't believe it. So, Captain Dan and Sam taught summer-school classes, too!

Oliver checked his watch. "Come on, Lilly, let's get our assignment for tomorrow and see what time we should report for duty."

Miley sighed as she remembered gloating to Lilly that she wouldn't have to take a summer-school class.

She remembered thanking her lucky stars

that she wouldn't have to do math until school started in the fall.

She remembered feeling absolutely joyous that she would have no academic duties whatsoever while on this vacation. . . .

What had she been thinking?

Miley watched glumly as Lilly and Oliver raced each other up the gangplank. "I can't believe Jackson *and* Lilly *and* Oliver are going to be spending time with Sam, and I'm not," she said. She caught Roxy's eye and added quickly, "Not whining! Just making an observation!"

"Seems like a smart girl like you could figure out a way to use this situation to your advantage," Roxy said.

"Really?" Miley considered this for a moment. "How?"

"I keep telling you, you got to think like a black belt," Roxy said. "Use your opponent's force against him. Then flip him over and— *pow!*—he's on his back like a bug, ready to be squashed!"

"Uh-huh." Miley wished Roxy would quit using karate metaphors. It made every life situation sound so scary . . . and painful. "Can you translate that into something a regular, non–karate-chopping person can understand?"

"I think you can figure it out if you open your eyes. Take a look at that." Roxy nodded toward the *Trueheart*, where Sam was showing Jackson how to raise a sail. Jackson said something that made Sam laugh.

Miley watched this heartwarming scene and felt nothing but burning jealousy. "Yeah?" she said. "So Sam and Jackson are already BFFs. So Sam can barely talk to me. So what?"

Roxy sighed an I-can't-believe-I-have-to-explain-this sigh. "So, get Jackson to invite the boy over to the cottage for hamburgers on the beach!" she said.

Miley's face lit up. "Roxy!" she said. "You are brilliant!"

"You know it," Roxy said smugly.

Miley was already pulling her cell phone out of her purse. "I'm calling Daddy right now and telling him to start building a bonfire," she said.

"Ask Lilly and Oliver if they want to come, too," Roxy suggested.

"Of course," Miley said, startled. Did Roxy really think she wouldn't? Roxy seemed to sense Miley's surprise. "That way it won't look so obvious that you're trying to get to know Sam," she explained. "In fact, maybe you should make it seem more like a party, invite a few other people, too. . . ."

Miley gave her a knowing smile. "Uh-huh. You got anybody special in mind?"

"Well," Roxy said, smiling back at her, "now that you mention it . . ."

Chapter Eight

So it's cheer up, my lads,
Let your hearts never fail,
For the bonny ship, The Diamond,
Goes a-fishing fo the whale.
   —"The Bonny Ship The Diamond*"*

The sun was just setting, turning the clouds on the horizon a deep gold and pink, when Miley and her father headed toward the water's edge to build the fire for their cookout.

Miley watched as her father lit the pyramid-shaped pile of wood that Jackson had built. She listened to the crackling of the flames and the hissing sound of the waves hitting the shore. A slight breeze lifted a strand of her brown hair. She tilted her head back and saw a single star twinkling in the deepening blue of the sky.

"Star light, star bright, first star I see tonight," she said softly.

Her father followed her gaze. "Make a wish, bud."

"Okay." After a second, she said, "There. I sure hope it comes true."

"Me, too, honey," he said. Then he looked more closely at Miley. "At least I think I do. What exactly did you wish for?"

She caught his eye and smiled. "Don't worry, Daddy," she said sweetly. "Just something that will make this vacation totally perfect."

When they returned to the kitchen, Miley and her dad found that Lilly, Oliver, Sam, and Captain Dan had all arrived. After everyone had been introduced, Mr. Stewart nodded toward the beat-up black leather case in Captain Dan's hand.

"If I had to take a guess," he said, "I'd say you were a fiddlin' man."

Captain Dan grinned. "Guilty as charged. I like to play a few tunes for my customers on the moonlight cruises. They seem to enjoy it . . . or at least they're smart enough to say they do until they're safely back on shore. And I thought a bonfire would be a good excuse. . . ."

"Oh, this family doesn't need an excuse for a hoedown," Mr. Stewart said, grinning. "Let me go grab my guitar. . . ."

He started toward the living room but was stopped by Roxy, who stood foursquare in the doorway. "Wait just one minute," she said. "That hoedown's gotta be put on hold, or none of us will be getting any supper."

Mr. Stewart wilted in the face of her stern look. "Of course, you're right," he said.

"Roxy's always right," she replied. "Now, let's get to work."

Within minutes, everyone had a job to do. Mr. Stewart was sent down to the beach to set up the grill for the burgers. Jackson was slicing onions and making a big deal about the tears running down his cheeks. Oliver was tossing a salad while Miley made the dressing. Lilly was stirring a pitcher of iced tea, and Sam was filling glasses with ice cubes. As for Captain Dan, he was cutting tomatoes into thin slices under Roxy's close supervision.

"Not too thin, or they won't hold up," she said. "Mr. Stewart's burgers tend to be on the chunky side."

The captain nodded and tried again. "How's this?" he asked.

Roxy inspected the newest slice and clucked her tongue. "Now that one's a little too thick," she said.

"Oh." Captain Dan examined the two slices, which to Miley looked practically identical. "Huh. Guess I just don't have the tomato touch," he said.

"Why don't we take these bad boys out on the porch and I'll show you my special slicing technique?" Roxy suggested. Within seconds, she'd gathered a bowl of tomatoes, a cutting board, and a knife, and was ushering Captain Dan out of the kitchen. As she passed Miley, she turned and gave her the ghost of a wink.

A short time later, Roxy herded the whole gang down to the beach, with drinks, paper plates, napkins, and platters piled high with food. A delicious smell let them know that the burgers were ready. And Mr. Stewart, his voice filled with pride, let them know that they were almost too good to eat.

"Take a bite of that," he said, sliding a patty onto Captain Dan's plate. "You won't often eat something that comes that close to perfection."

As everyone served themselves, Miley glanced around the bonfire, scoping out the seating situation. Earlier in the afternoon, Jackson and Oliver had dragged several logs over for people to sit on and placed them in a rough circle around the fire.

Now Miley hung back so that she would be served after Sam. It was only good manners, she told herself. She waited until Sam took his seat on the end of one log, then she casually sat down at the other end, leaving just enough room between them so that it wouldn't look as if she were trying to make some kind of move.

As she settled herself, however, Miley saw Sam glance over. Of course, he looked away immediately . . . but still. Even a little glance showed progress.

Maybe tonight's the night he'll finally talk to me all on his own, Miley thought.

But then Sam started arranging lettuce and tomato slices on his burger with such intense concentration that he seemed to have forgotten her very existence.

Or maybe I need to help him along, she thought.

She cleared her throat. "So, Sam," she said, "I'm sure you know a lot about the stars from all your sailing. It might be nice to take a little walk later. Maybe you could point out some constellations. . . ."

"Uh, yeah," he said as he squeezed ketchup onto his bun with the laserlike focus of a heart surgeon.

Come on, work with me here! Miley thought irritably. I just gave you the best lead-in of all time.

"I know the Big Dipper is supposed to be easy to spot," she went on. "But when I try to find it, I'm not even sure what part of the sky I should be looking at—"

"Oh, I can help you with that, Miley," said Oliver cheerfully, walking over to join them.

"Thanks, Oliver," Miley said, her tone frosty as she shot him a severe look. Anyone else would have understood that tone of voice; anyone else would have gotten a clue from her pointed glare; anyone else would have known enough to excuse himself and leave Miley alone with Sam. . . .

But Oliver was not anyone else. And he proved it just then by managing to trip over basically nothing.

"Whoa!" he shouted, windmilling his arms as he tried to recover his balance and keep his food from sliding off his plate. Finally, he plopped down next to Miley, panting slightly.

He grinned at her. "Whew! Made it."

Miley's shoulders sagged. "Wonderful."

She took a disgruntled bite of her burger and tried to listen in to the conversation Jackson and Sam were now having.

"Hey, there's a late showing of that old movie *Space Vampires* at the theater in town," Jackson said to Sam. "Want to check it out?"

"Sure," Sam said. "That's a classic. And I've only ever seen it on TV. It would be awesome to see it on the big screen."

At least now I know Sam likes horror movies, Miley thought. Okay, this wasn't *great* news—she hated horror movies—but this was more than he ever would have told her.

Miley lost track of the next few exchanges that Sam had with Jackson, however, because all of a sudden Oliver started chattering about some book he'd found in a store in town. Miley tried to shut out what he was saying, but it was hard when Oliver was practically shouting across the bonfire at Captain Dan.

"Hey, Captain Dan, look at this book I bought today." Oliver pulled a small volume out of his pocket and waved it in the air. "*Steering by the Stars.* Cool, huh? I figured I should study up on the constellations in case I'm ever adrift at sea during the night and my ship's directional equipment is broken and everyone on board is relying on me to guide them to safety."

"Good plan," Captain Dan said. "It's always best to be prepared for the worst."

"Well, if we're going to be steering by the stars, I figure I'd better know what they are,"

Oliver said, a trifle smugly. Then his face darkened. "And I haven't been sleeping so well lately, so I have a lot more time to read."

"What's the matter, Oliver?" Jackson asked teasingly. "Are you having those nightmares about the killer teddy bear again?"

"Hey, I haven't had that dream since I was six," Oliver protested. "And that teddy bear was *terrifying*, for your information. But now"—he exchanged a look with Lilly—"it's more a case of mysterious noises in the night."

Lilly rolled her eyes. "I told you a dozen times, that was the toilet running."

"You just keep telling yourself that, Lilly," Oliver replied. "But I'm locking my door just the same."

Mr. Stewart was listening to this with an amused expression. "What's got you nervous as a june bug, Oliver?"

"Please." Lilly threw her paper plate into the fire. "Don't encourage him or his imagination."

"I'm not imagining anything," Oliver said.

He lowered his voice to a dramatic whisper. "Lilly's great-aunt Agatha is a very sinister woman."

"Eccentric," Lilly insisted.

"This morning, she made a point of showing me the lilac bush beside the house," Oliver told the others, throwing out his hands as if he'd just scored a winning point.

Roxy shrugged. "So the woman's proud of her garden."

"And then she told me that the root is a deadly poison!" Oliver went on, his voice getting higher. "And that I should be careful not to get any in my tea, because the taste can't be detected! And that it was used in a famous murder on this very island back in 1902!"

Captain Dan was chuckling. "I wouldn't get too worked up if I were you," he said. "Agatha Kilpatrick is a might odd, but she's lived here all her life. As far as I know, she doesn't have any bodies buried in the basement."

But Oliver refused to be comforted. "As. Far.

As. You. Know," he repeated meaningfully.

"Oh, honestly!" Lilly said. "I wish you'd calm down, Oliver. This is just like the time you watched that scary movie marathon on TV and then called me at two in the morning because you thought a zombie was trying to get in your window!"

Jackson chuckled. "Dude, really?" he said, grinning at Oliver. "I mean, everyone knows zombies usually just break down the front door."

"Laugh now," Oliver said. "But when the worst happens, I just want one thing. I want you all to admit that I was right. There is something strange going on in that house. I can feel it in my bones."

Roxy shook her head. "Well, why don't you stir those bones and help me carry our dessert down here?" she suggested. "Nothing like doing a chore or two to get your mind off your fears."

As Oliver followed Roxy up to the cottage, Miley tuned in to Jackson and Sam once again.

Unbelievably, they had gone back to talking about that lame movie!

"Oh, and you know another great scene?" Sam was saying. "That one where the vampire climbs up the wall to get into the old farmhouse!"

"Scariest part of the whole movie," Jackson agreed through a mouthful of potato salad. "Especially when the vampire's head pops up and he flashes his fangs."

"Dude, totally," Sam agreed. "I screamed the first time I saw that, and I'm man enough to admit it."

As Sam and Jackson continued recounting scene after scene from *Space Vampires*, Miley stared into the crackling fire and tried to enjoy her meal. But it was no good; she had lost her appetite completely.

She'd tried everything she could think of to be friendly and fun and flirtatious with Sam, but nothing was working. He could hardly make himself look at her, let alone talk to her!

And now . . . oh, no! Now Sam was leaning forward to talk to Lilly, who was sitting on the other side of Jackson.

"How was your first day of class?" he asked her. "Are you completely confused yet?"

Lilly grinned. "Let's just say I'm doing better than I did in algebra last year," she said. "Of course, considering my algebra grade, that's not saying much."

Sam nodded sympathetically. "Don't worry, it starts making sense eventually," he said. "What tripped you up today?"

As Lilly started rambling on—something about measuring angles with a sextant that wasn't worth listening to—Miley took a big bite of potato salad and seethed.

There Sam sat, chatting away with Lilly—Lilly!—as if she were the most fascinating person in the world! And he had spent even more time talking to Jackson. Jackson, who had never said anything of interest to anyone in his entire life!

Miley glumly crumpled her paper napkin and threw it in the fire. She had had such high hopes for this beach cookout and now she couldn't wait for it to end.

Well, here was Oliver, carrying raspberry cobbler, followed by Roxy carrying a stack of bowls. Pretty soon, they'd be eating dessert, then Sam and Captain Dan would leave, and this whole miserable evening would finally be over. . . .

Just then, a flash of silver slid down the sky.

"Oh, look!" Lilly cried out. "A shooting star! Make a wish, everybody!"

Miley gave the sky a baleful look. She wasn't going to trust her wishes to stars any-more. They obviously didn't really care about the hopes and dreams of all the little people down on the ground.

"You might be interested to know that the star came from the same part of the sky as the constellation Orion," Oliver said. He pointed to the sky. "See those three stars in a row?

That's Orion's belt. Now, once you find that, you can find the star called Sirius very easily. And once you find the star Sirius—"

"Yeah, we know, you'll be able to make it back to port even if your distress flares are damp and your radio is broken," Miley said, standing up hastily. She caught Lilly's eye. "Hey, Lilly, I think we have kitchen duty tonight. Why don't we get started on these dishes?"

Lilly glanced up, her mouth half-open in surprise. "But I thought I'd go back for seconds—"

"You can eat later," Miley said, pulling Lilly to her feet. "Come on!"

She and Lilly collected an armful of plates and headed toward the cottage. As soon as they reached the kitchen, Miley hissed to Lilly, "Listen! I need your help."

Lilly turned on the hot water and squirted a generous amount of liquid soap into the sink. "I already said I'd wash," she replied. "But you've got to dry. You promised."

Miley rolled her eyes. "Yes, fine," she said. "But that's not what I'm talking about. I need your help with Sam."

Lilly stopped putting dirty dishes into the water in order to turn to Miley and stare. "You're kidding. Why should you need my help? He's so nice. All you have to do is flirt a little to let him know you're interested."

"I've tried," Miley said. "Believe me. Nothing's happening."

"Really?" Lilly looked thoughtful. "Hmm. That's weird."

"Maybe he's just not that into me," Miley said forlornly.

"Oh, come on." Lilly gave her a friendly nudge with her elbow. "Why would you think that?"

Miley put down the dish towel and began ticking off points on her fingers. "One, he hardly ever looks at me. Two, he hardly ever talks to me. And three, he never laughs at my jokes."

"No one laughs at your jokes," Lilly pointed out, trying to tease her into a better mood. But Miley wasn't interested in being teased, or in changing her mood.

She shook her head. "Face it, Lilly. I've got no game."

Miley moved to the kitchen window and peered out. The bonfire's flames were dying down, but there was enough light for her to see that Sam was talking with her dad and Captain Dan. And he seemed pretty enthusiastic about the conversation, too—he was even waving his hands in the air to make a point.

"Why won't Sam even look at me?" she wondered out loud. "It just doesn't make sense."

As she spoke, Roxy entered the kitchen, carrying another stack of dishes. "Now, don't worry so much about that Sam," she said. "After all, boys are mysterious creatures. Sometimes they act sweet even though they're really rascals, sometimes they act cool as cucumbers even though they feel the exact opposite, and sometimes they act completely squirrely for no good reason at all."

"Thanks, Roxy," Miley said with a slight edge to her voice. "Now that you've explained all that, I understand boys *so much better.*"

"Hey, if you ever listened to Roxy, you'd understand a lot more than boys," her bodyguard said, shrugging. "But do you listen? Nope. Poor old Roxy's pearls of wisdom are completely ignored—"

"No, they aren't; I hang on every word you say," Miley said, even as she was turning back to Lilly. "Okay, what about this idea? Maybe I can tag along when Jackson and Sam go to that horror movie."

"You hate horror movies," Lilly reminded her. "They make you scream—"

"And grab the person sitting next to me," Miley countered brightly. "Which, in this case, could be Sam."

"You'll be having nightmares about space vampires for weeks," Lilly said.

"I'm willing to make sacrifices for what could be the beginning of a beautiful friendship," Miley answered.

"*You* may be, but *I'm* the one who'll wake up when you start yelling in the night," Roxy said firmly.

"All I want is a little summer romance." Miley sighed. "Just a little walk on the beach. Is that too much to ask?"

"Whoa there, Miss Summer Romance." Roxy lifted her foot. "See this?"

Miley and Lilly stared at the sizable purple sneaker Roxy was waggling in the air. "Yeah?"

"Good." Roxy stomped the floor. "That's me putting my foot down. I need my beauty sleep, and so do you. Remember, you've got another photo shoot tomorrow morning."

"Oh, okay," Miley said, crestfallen. "I guess you're right."

Roxy patted her on the arm as she left the kitchen. "Don't look so sad," she said.

"But we only have a few more days on the

island," Miley said forlornly, watching Roxy go out the door.

"Well, then we'd better make the most of them," Lilly told her. "Come on, let's hurry up with the dishes and get back to the bonfire."

By the time Miley and Lilly had finished in the kitchen and returned to the beach, Mr. Stewart had started tuning his guitar and Captain Dan was warming up his fiddle.

"Does everybody know this one?" Mr. Stewart asked. He started playing "Rocky Top."

Everyone sang along. The firelight lit their faces with a warm glow and made the dark night beyond the circle look even deeper and more mysterious. This must be what it was like centuries ago, Miley thought, when everyone gathered around the fire in the evening with their friends and family. There was a feeling of togetherness and camaraderie, of holding back the night through smiles and songs, which made the music seem like more than just entertainment. It felt as if they were all connecting with each other in some more profound and soulful way. Miley felt warm and happy and fond of everyone . . . even Jackson.

She glanced at Sam and noticed that he was singing quite softly. In fact, she thought he might be just mouthing the words.

Probably can't carry a tune, Miley thought, a little smugly. Probably embarrassed to have us hear his voice.

And just like that, an idea flashed into her mind. So Sam wasn't interested in her? Maybe she just needed to impress him. . . . And what better way to impress him than with her own voice?!

Immediately, she found herself singing a little more loudly. Her voice no longer blended in with the other voices. It rose, high and clear, above them. And Miley was no longer just singing along with her friends and family, lost in the music. Now there was a part of her that was separate, listening to herself, judging how she sounded just as she would have in a recording studio.

Not bad, she thought, but the delivery's a little bland. Maybe I should add some vibrato. . . .

She did, and it worked. Now the other voices were more of a background chorus, supporting her as she took the lead. Miley smiled, really enjoying herself now and totally in her element as she sang the last line of the song. . . .

Then she suddenly realized that she was singing by herself.

She looked around the circle of faces. Captain Dan and Sam looked impressed. Her dad and Roxy seemed faintly disapproving. And Lilly, Oliver, and Jackson were all rolling their eyes with the identical expression that said, Get over yourself, already!

"Um, sorry," she said. "I guess I got carried away."

"I can see why," Captain Dan said. "You have a great voice."

Miley's spirits lifted at the compliment, but she smiled modestly. "Oh, no, not really—"

"You know who else has a good voice?" Captain Dan interrupted.

Jackson snickered, and Miley shot him an irritated look. "No, who?" she said.

"Sam over there," Captain Dan said. He raised his voice slightly. "Hey, Sam. Why don't we do 'A Hundred Years Ago' for these folks?"

"Oh. Um. Well." Sam looked mortified.

Captain Dan played a few sprightly notes on his fiddle. "He's the star of every cruise," he said, ignoring Sam's discomfort, "but he's real shy about it. Has to be coaxed into singing every time . . . then once he gets going, he won't stop. And let me tell you something else for free, the girls really like to hear him, too—"

"Okay, okay, I'll sing," Sam said, clearly hoping this would make Captain Dan stop talking.

"Embarrassing him works pretty well, too," Captain Dan said with a wink. He put his bow to the strings and began to play.

It was a lively, jaunty tune that danced through the night like a ghost from the past. Sam cleared his throat, looking a little nervous, but after the first few notes, he took a deep breath and started to sing.

A hundred years is a very long time,
Ho, yes, ho!
A hundred years is a very long time,
A hundred years ago.

They used to think that pigs could fly
Ho, yes, ho!
I don't believe it, no, not I.
A hundred years ago.
They thought the moon was made of cheese.
Ho, yes, ho!

You can believe it if you please.
A hundred years ago.

They thought the stars were set a-light,
Ho, yes, ho!
By some good angel every night,
A hundred years ago.

A hundred years is a very long time,
Ho, yes, ho!
A hundred years is a very long time,
A hundred years ago.

Miley felt a shiver of surprise. Sam's singing voice was deeper than his speaking voice and remarkably confident. She blushed in the dark at her smug thoughts about how he probably couldn't carry a tune. In fact, he hit every note perfectly. Not only that, but his breath control was amazing. Once he got warmed up and swung into the second chorus, he even started adding a little personality to the song.

And he was smiling. He seemed lost in the music. Relaxed. Confident. Miley could sense what he was feeling, because it was what she experienced herself every time she went onstage. There were the nerves, of course, right before the show opened. Her dad always told her that they helped a singer give her best performance. But then, as soon as she launched into her first song, she forgot about the butterflies in her stomach and started to have fun.

Miley tilted her head to one side and watched Sam even more closely. She had always read in magazines that the best way to get to know someone was to talk about a common interest. Surely, if Sam was a great singer and she was a pop star—not that she would tell him that, of course, but she'd done pretty well singing around the bonfire tonight, so he had to see that she had skills—well, surely, they could at least get a conversation going.

Miley's dad caught her eye and grinned. He was already tapping his toes; now he began to clap to the beat. The others soon joined in, and by the time Sam reached the third chorus they all knew the words well enough to sing along. The song ended with Captain Dan playing a rapid run of notes on his fiddle, then flourishing his bow in the air as everyone applauded.

"Great job, son," Mr. Stewart said to Sam. "You sound like you've been singing for a while."

Sam ducked his head at the praise, shy again now that the song was over. "All my life," he said, in a voice so quiet it was almost drowned out by the sound of the surf. "My parents belong to a folk-singing group. I grew up listening to sea chanteys. I didn't even know the words to any pop songs until I got to fifth grade." He stopped abruptly, as if afraid he'd said too much. "Pretty nerdy, I know."

"No, no, not at all . . ." Miley started to say, hoping to reassure him.

But Roxy started talking right over her. "I'd say those songs are pretty romantic," she said, cutting her eyes to Captain Dan. "Makes me feel like I've gone back in time to the days of pirates on the high seas! Mm-mm-mm. All those dashing men with their flouncy white shirts and their wicked grins—"

"And the eye patches and the peg legs," Miley put in, rolling her eyes. "And no baths! Remember that part, Roxy."

"Hygiene would be a problem," Roxy admitted. "But nothing that a little guidance from Roxy wouldn't fix."

Mr. Stewart shook his head. "You'd try to whip anybody into shape, wouldn't you?"

"Never met my match yet," Roxy boasted.

"I can believe that," Captain Dan said, laughing. "In fact, I pity the pirate who ever tries to cross you."

Roxy's smile flashed in the moonlight. "You got that right."

"So, what's our next number?" Mr. Stewart asked. "Do we all know 'Shine On, Harvest Moon'? Yeah? Then here we go!"

He swung into the song, with Captain Dan fiddling along. As everyone began singing, Miley watched the moon's silver reflection dance across the water. And even though Sam *still* wasn't looking at her and she was beginning to doubt that he ever would, she felt a warm glow of happiness inside.

 Chapter Nine

Oh, for a soft and gentle wind,
I heard a fair one cry,
But give me the roaring breeze,
And the white waves heaving high.
　　　—"A Wet Sheet and a Flowing Sea"

The next morning, after a restless night, Oliver woke up early and made his way downstairs to the kitchen. No one else seemed to be up yet, so he filled the teakettle with water and put it on the stove to heat. As he started for the pantry to get a box of cereal, he felt something lithe and furry slip between his feet.

"*Ahhh!*" he yelled, jumping onto a chair. He looked down to see Marlowe coolly staring up at him. Oliver could have sworn that there was a sardonic gleam in the cat's green eyes.

"What are you lookin' at?" he said, trying for some action-hero bluster.

Of course, the cat couldn't understand him. Oliver knew that. Still, when Marlowe gave one slow, thoughtful, blink in response, he felt a shiver run down his spine.

He stepped down off the chair. "You don't scare me, Marlowe," he said, backing away gingerly. The cat continued to stare at him, swishing his tail back and forth in a rather menacing manner. "You don't scare me one little bit—"

"Who doesn't scare you?" a voice said.

"Ahhh!" For the second time in less than five minutes, Oliver screamed. This time, however, he turned to see Lilly watching him. Her eyes flicked past him, and she grinned.

"Don't tell me that you're talking to Marlowe now," she said. "Maybe Great-aunt Agatha isn't the only crazy one around here."

"I was not talking to that cat," Oliver said with great dignity. "More like laying down the law."

"Oh, good." Lilly opened the refrigerator and grabbed a carton of orange juice. "'Cause, you know, *threatening* a cat is so much more understandable than *chatting* with a cat."

"Hmph." Oliver decided to change the subject. He eyed Lilly narrowly. "You sound pretty calm this morning, considering how you freaked out last night when the bulb in your night-light burned out."

Lilly shrugged as she poured a glass of juice. "Everything looks better in the morning," she said. "The sun is shining, I've had a good night's sleep, and in the clear light of day I can see that there's absolutely no reason to be nervous."

"Really," Oliver said. "Have you seen your great-aunt yet this morning?"

"Yeah, she's already in the garden," Lilly answered. "I saw her out my window."

Oliver eased his way over to the kitchen window and peered out from behind the curtain. "In the garden, huh?" he asked. "Doing what, I wonder?"

Lilly rolled her eyes. "Digging up a flower bed, I think," she said. "Would you stop already with the private-detective act? It's getting kind of old."

Oliver turned his gaze from the backyard (where the flowers were nodding in the sun, and everything looked completely normal) and turned it on his poor, dear, deluded friend Lilly. "And why, do you suppose, would she want to dig up a flower bed?" he asked patiently.

"Well, I'm not a gardener," Lilly said. "But if I had to guess, I'd say she maybe, oh, I don't know—wanted to plant some flowers in it?"

"Or plant something else," he said darkly. *"Like a body."*

"Did I hear someone say something about planting?" a cool, amused voice said.

"Ahhh!" Oliver screamed for the third time.

He turned to see Mrs. Kilpatrick standing in the doorway, holding a small bouquet and a vicious-looking pair of pruning shears.

"What do you think of my flowers?" she asked, holding out the bouquet. "I make my own special bouquet every morning: belladonna, foxglove, and jimsonweed." She smiled dryly. "Delightful, aren't they?"

But Oliver couldn't keep his eyes off those pruning shears. Not only were the blades sharp, but they were marked with a sinister dark stain. In fact, if he squinted just a little, it almost looked like . . . dried blood!

His eyes widened, and his head began to swim. For a moment, he thought he was going to faint. . . .

"Oliver? Oliver!"

Lilly pushed him into a chair and made him hang his head between his knees. "Sorry," she said to her great-aunt. "He gets like this sometimes when he, uh, hasn't had enough to eat."

"Poor boy!" Mrs. Kilpatrick put the shears

on the table. Oliver caught a glimpse of them out of the corner of his eye and shuddered. "Let me fix you some toast right away."

She popped some bread into an ancient toaster and was getting butter from the refrigerator when she was interrupted by the sound of the doorbell.

"Oh, that must be the delivery man," she said. "Excuse me."

As soon as she left the kitchen, Lilly leaned down and whispered to Oliver, "What in the world is *wrong* with you?"

"*Shh!*" he whispered back. "Stay calm! Act normal!"

"I am calm, and I am acting normal!" she hissed. "You're the one who's acting like a crazy person!"

"Did you notice how she made a point of telling us what those flowers were?" Oliver said, forgetting to keep his voice down. "Belladonna! Foxglove! Jimsonweed!"

Lilly shook her head in confusion. "So?"

"So, those flowers all have one thing in common." He leaned over to speak directly in her ear. "They're all poison! *Poison*, do you hear me?"

"Hey!" Lilly complained, wiping off her ear. "Watch the spit!"

"I'm just trying to get you to see that something very strange is going on here," Oliver said. "You can thank me later."

"I wasn't planning on thanking you at all," Lilly snarled. "I was planning on telling you"—she yelled in his ear—*"you're crazy!"*

"Hey!" He jumped back, grabbed a napkin, and dried off his ear. "What was that?"

"Payback." Lilly stood up and grabbed her purse. "Now come on. If we don't get going, we'll be late for class."

"Aaaggh!" As Miley stood on the dock, ready to go on board a sailing ship for the final day of the photo shoot, a sudden gust of wind whipped her blond hair across her face.

She reached up to make sure her Hannah wig was still on her head, and another gust almost pushed her over. As she struggled to stay upright on her three-inch stiletto heels, the wind changed direction and this time blew her skirt up around her waist. "Roxy! Help!"

"I got you baby," Roxy said, rushing over to pull the skirt down.

Miley pushed her hair out of her eyes. "Remind me why I have to wear a ball gown for a shoot that's going to take place on a ship?"

Roxy shrugged. "You got me. That Jeremy kept going on and on about 'the contrast between elegance and simplicity,' but I stopped listening after about ten minutes." She shook her head. "That boy sure can talk."

Miley glanced down at the dress. The bodice was emerald green satin, with an abundance of ruffles. The skirt was a red and green–striped satin, and there were so many yards of material in it that she felt as if she were going to fly away every time the wind blew.

"If the ship loses a sail, they can always use the skirt of this dress," she muttered. She took three tottering steps toward the gang-plank, almost fell, and grabbed for the nearest wooden post.

"Hannah, darling, you look adorable," Jeremy said as he came bounding up. "Very chic! Very modern! Very now!"

"Really?" Miley said, looking down at herself with a trace of doubt. " 'Cause I feel like a giant Christmas ornament."

At that moment, Josie swooped in to touch up Hannah's makeup, and Sabrina darted over to make an adjustment to her hem.

Sabrina sniffed. "This happens to be an original gown from François du Lyon's new collection," she said. "It's worth more than all the other outfits in this photo shoot combined."

"Oh." Miley gazed down at her striped skirt and tried to give it a little more respect, but it was no use. She still felt like she belonged on a Christmas tree.

"Okay, everyone, all aboard," Jeremy cried out, clapping his hands.

Miley inched her way up the gangplank and gingerly stepped over the side of the ship. As she walked to the railing, she saw a familiar ship nearby.

It was the *Trueheart*. She could see Lilly and Oliver, along with a handful of other students, listening to Captain Dan lecture. She spotted Jackson in the back of the ship. Unbelievably, he appeared to be scrubbing the deck. Miley grinned to herself and resolved to remind him of this the next time he claimed he couldn't mop the kitchen floor because of his bad back.

Then she heard Captain Dan's voice boom across the water. "Raise the mainsail!"

"Aye, aye, Captain!" Sam yelled back.

The sail was raised, and it suddenly billowed in the wind.

There was a small cheer from the students. Sam waved in acknowledgment. Even from a distance, she could see his easy grin.

The memory of how uncomfortable he always looked around Miley flashed through her mind, and her shoulders drooped. She wished she could sit down and put her head in her hands, but there didn't seem to be many clean spots, and Sabrina's sharp comment about the cost of the dress still echoed in her head. Miley sighed and settled for leaning against the railing.

"You're not getting seasick, are you?" a voice said behind her. She turned to see Jeremy watching her shrewdly. "After all, we're only a few yards from shore."

"Oh, no, I'm fine," Miley said with a bright smile. She noticed that while she'd been looking for Sam, the crew of her own ship had cast off, and they were now moving slowly but steadily away from the dock.

"We're just going to sail out a little way, then we'll drop anchor," Jeremy explained. "That way, Chad can get shots of you with the open sea and sky as a background. In fact, why don't you come to the front of the boat and I'll show you where we'd like you to stand. . . ."

As Miley followed Chad to the prow, she couldn't help glancing over at the *Trueheart*. By the time her ship dropped anchor, the *Trueheart* was just fifty yards away. Miley looked wistfully at the students on board. They looked like they were gaving a great time. . . .

"Psst!" someone hissed.

Miley swung her head around. She spotted Roxy hiding behind the galley.

"Hannah! Come here!" Roxy called softly, gesturing for her to come over.

Miley inched her way over. "What's wrong?" she asked. "You look like you're in hiding."

"I am!" Roxy said. "Who do you see on that ship over there?"

Miley turned to follow her gaze. "Well, Sam, of course . . ."

"Will you forget about that boy for one measly second?" Roxy snapped. "Who's he with?"

Miley squinted at the *Trueheart*. "Jackson. Lilly. Oliver. All those summer-school students—"

"Girl, you have an amazing talent for missing the obvious!" Roxy said. "Sam is there with Captain Dan. And they both know me *as Miley's friend*—not as Hannah's bodyguard."

Miley's eyes widened. "Oh, no. If they see you—"

"Bingo." Roxy snapped her fingers. "They'll wonder what I'm doing here. I've got to stay out of sight until we get back to land." She sighed heavily. "I'm sorry. I know it's a terrible dereliction of my duties."

"Don't worry, I think I can manage this on my own," Miley said reassuringly. "After all, there aren't any crazed fans or rabid paparazzi out here in the middle of the ocean."

Roxy still looked worried, but she nodded. "You're right," she said. "What could possibly go wrong?"

"Okay, everybody, let's get going!" Jeremy clapped his hands, and instantly a scurry of photo-shoot activity began. Chad's assistant double-checked his light meter, Josie powdered Hannah's nose one more time, and Sabrina pursed her lips as she brushed off Hannah's skirt. . . .

Suddenly, Miley noticed Oliver raising a pair of binoculars and scanning the horizon. As the binoculars swept past Miley's ship, he started in surprise, then gave a little wave. Miley waved back. Then she noticed the other students beginning to move toward the railing. Some of them were pointing at her and waving.

This, at least, was familiar territory for Hannah Montana. Miley smiled and waved to her fans. Even as she did so, she couldn't help but notice that Sam had climbed down from the rigging and was in the middle of doing a chore. But even he raised his head to see what the commotion was about. A few moments later, he drifted over to watch the photo shoot in progress.

Miley's spirits lifted. True, Sam didn't know he was watching *her*, Miley Stewart. But still, it was nice to finally catch his eye. . . .

"Turn this way, Hannah," Chad called out. He was looking through the viewfinder of his camera with an intense expression on his face. "Now glance over your shoulder. That's it. Chin up a bit. Good. Big smile. Excellent. Try putting your hands on your hips. Very good . . ."

As Miley followed his directions automatically, she let her mind drift.

So. She now, at long last, had Sam's attention. Even though she couldn't let him know who she really was, surely there was a way to use this situation to her advantage.

"Lean out over the railing," Chad said, still

clicking away. "Turn to the right. Let's get the wind blowing your hair."

Miley tossed her head so that her hair flew up into the air.

"Fantastic!" Chad yelled. "Do that again!"

Her mood brightened even more. She had forgotten how much fun it was to pose for the camera, to be playful and flirty as the lens captured every moment—especially with the crew of the *Trueheart* watching, enthralled at this peek at a glamorous celebrity shoot.

Delighted with herself, Miley grabbed a rope that was attached to the deck and stepped up onto the railing.

"Whoa, watch yourself!" Roxy yelled.

Miley glanced over at the galley where Roxy was still hiding and smiled. "I'm fine!" she yelled back.

Holding onto the rope with her left hand, she flung her right hand into the air. Chad was moving around on the deck below her, trying to get shots from all different angles.

A small cheer floated across the water from the deck of the *Trueheart*.

Miley jauntily grabbed the end of another rope with her right hand, then let go with her left, so she was now balanced on the railing with her back to the sea below.

"That's wonderful!" Chad said. "Now, can you try lifting your right leg so that we see more of your skirt. . . ."

Of course, Miley thought, excitement fizzing through her veins. I can do anything!

With that thought, she leaned back slightly to do a high kick. But between one breath and the next, her hand slipped on the rope and she lost her balance.

And then she was gone. . . .

 *Chapter Ten*

Cape Cod girls ain't got no combs;
They brush their hair with codfish bones.
                    —"Cape Cod Girls"

The cold seawater closed over Miley's head. She squeezed her eyes tight against the salty sting and tried to swim toward the surface, but the yards of material in her skirt were now sodden and heavy. She barely managed to get her head above water and breathe in a quick gasp of air before sinking again.

She kicked her feet desperately and discovered that her skirt had twisted around her legs, limiting her movement. In her mind's eye, she saw the last glimpse she'd had of the ship before she went under. Miley hadn't seen Roxy. Maybe she hadn't seen Miley fall from where she was hiding. . . .

But even so, Roxy must have heard the splash. . . . Surely she'd dive in and save her. . . .

Then, just as Miley thought her lungs were going to burst, she felt strong arms around her. The next second she was pulled to the surface.

She took in a huge, gasping breath and blinked up at the blue sky. At first her eyes were so dazzled by the sunlight reflecting off the water that she couldn't see who was holding her. In fact, she was so grateful to be able to breathe that she really didn't care.

That is, not until she finally turned her head and came nose-to-nose with . . . Sam.

His hair was slicked down with seawater, and he was panting, tired from the effort of keeping them both afloat. Still, he managed to smile at her. "Don't worry," he said. "I've got you."

"Thanks," she said fervently. Then, feeling that she somehow hadn't sounded quite grateful enough, she added, "Really, thank you, thank you, thank you. . . ."

"That's okay," Sam said, managing to laugh. "It's all in a day's work for a sailor. Now we just need to get you back on dry land."

They both turned to see a rope ladder being lowered to them from the deck of the ship.

"Think you could climb that?" Sam asked.

Looking up, Miley suddenly realized how very high the side of the ship was. She shook her head. "I don't think so," she said. "This dress weighs a ton."

Sam glanced over Miley's shoulder and his face brightened. "Hey, Nate!" he yelled as a smaller sailboat edged near them.

"Looks like you need a lift." A teen boy with brown hair and a wide smile leaned over the side of the boat, offering his hand to Miley. "Grab hold, I'll pull you in."

"Oh, but what about S—" Just in time, Miley remembered that Hannah Montana did not know Sam Bliss's name. "Saving us both?"

Nate laughed. "Sam could swim to shore if he wanted to. Anyway, women and children first."

"That's the rule of the sea," Sam agreed, treading water and looking as comfortable as if he were on land.

Miley put her hand in Nate's and allowed herself to be hauled over the side of the boat. She ended up flopping onto the deck like a freshly caught tuna and was suddenly very glad Sam couldn't see this part of her rescue.

By the time Nate pulled Sam out of the water, Miley had checked that her blond wig was still in place and was wringing out her skirt.

Sam came over to sit beside her. "Nate will take us to the dock," he said. "Then you can change out of your, um . . ."

She looked down at herself and started laughing. "Well, it used to be a ball gown," she said. "But it looks kind of the worse for wear." She suddenly felt self-conscious. "I'm sure I do, too—"

"You look fine," Sam said. "Just a little damp, that's all."

"Thanks," Miley, still as Hannah, said shyly. She looked down at the deck, searching for something to say. Here she'd been dying to have a conversation with Sam for days, and here he was actually talking, and . . . her mind was totally blank!

Then she heard Lilly yell, "Glad you're okay, Hannah!" and looked up to see that they were sailing past the *Trueheart*. Oliver gave her a thumbs-up. Some of the other students cheered. As she grinned and waved to them, she remembered that, even though *Miley* might be at a loss for words, right now she wasn't Miley . . . she was Hannah Montana.

So, she gave Sam a flirtatious glance and

her warmest smile. "Well, now that you've saved me from drowning, just like a real hero . . . what's your name?"

"I can't believe it!" Miley stood in the middle of her bedroom at the Bumblebee Inn, dripping all over the carpet. "I simply can't believe it!"

"Well, while you're busy not believing whatever it is you don't believe, why don't you get that wet dress off," Roxy suggested. "You'll catch a cold if you don't get into some dry clothes, pronto."

Miley pulled off her Hannah wig and dropped it in a bedraggled heap on the floor. Then she peeled off her sodden clothes and put on her cozy fleece bathrobe.

"The entire time we were in that sailboat, Sam was totally friendly and nice!" she said, toweling her hair dry. "He said more than two words at a time! He even smiled!"

"What's the problem with that?" Roxy asked. She plucked a long slimy strand of kelp off Miley's skirt. "Ooh, this is one nasty ball gown."

"The problem is that he has *never* been that way with me! I mean, with Miley." She slumped down on her bed, frowning. "But with Hannah, it was all 'have you ever gone sailing before' and 'do you want to know the names of all the different sails' and 'I really like your songs.'"

"Sounds like the boy's a Hannah fan," Roxy commented.

Miley fell back on her bed, pulled a pillow over her face and groaned. "Who cares if he's a Hannah fan? He hates Miley!"

"Hate is a pretty strong word," Roxy said mildly. "And if he likes Hannah, he's bound to like Miley . . . I mean, considering that you're both the same person."

"Hmmph." Miley tossed the pillow to the floor and stared at the ceiling. "How do I keep getting into these situations?"

"Baby, I gotta say something," Roxy said.

Miley felt a mild rush of panic. She had never seen Roxy look so somber. "What is it?" she asked.

Roxy sighed deeply. "I've been derelict in my duty," she said in a confessional tone. "I've let you down."

"What are you talking about?" Miley asked, completely confused. "You've never let me down! Never ever!"

This just seemed to make Roxy feel worse. She shook her head sorrowfully. "I never did in the past," she said. "But today, well . . ."

She looked right at Miley, her eyes glistening slightly. "I'm sorry. You fell in the ocean and I . . . I didn't jump in to save you."

Miley sat up straight, the better to stare at Roxy. "Is that what all this soap opera's about?" she asked, so relieved that she felt like laughing. She couldn't laugh, though. She couldn't even smile, not when Roxy was so clearly upset.

"Come on, Roxy! You couldn't jump in

after me. Captain Dan and Sam would have seen you, my secret identity would have been exposed, and I wouldn't be able to live a normal life anymore. So maybe you weren't protecting Hannah, but you were protecting Miley."

"But my job is to protect Hannah Montana," Roxy insisted. "And let's face it . . . I heard you land in the drink and . . . I froze." She shook her head mournfully. "I gotta tell your daddy about this. And then I gotta resign."

"What?" Miley said.

"If Captain Dan didn't know me, I would have been in the water in a flash," Roxy insisted. "There's no way around it. I'm no kind of bodyguard for you."

"But then I was rescued by Sam!" Miley smiled brightly. "You see? Everything turns out for the best."

"Huh." Roxy gave her a considering look. "That logic smells a little fishy."

Miley smiled at her. "I think that's my dress."

Roxy couldn't help smiling as Miley went on to press her case. "Please, Roxy. You can't leave me. You just can't!"

"Okay, okay," Roxy said, laughing. Then her expression turned serious. "But I promise, I'll make it up to you."

"Really?" Miley hummed thoughtfully as visions of Roxy doing the dishes instead of her danced in her head. "Well, in that case, maybe you'd like a few ideas—"

But Roxy wasn't listening. She had started pacing purposefully back and forth across the room. "From now on, you won't be able to move an inch without me."

Miley felt a flutter of panic. She'd experienced Roxy's overprotectiveness before, and it always put a serious crimp in her plans. "Um, Roxy? That really won't be necessary. . . ."

"I will stick to you like a tick on a hound dog," Roxy went on.

"I really don't think that's a good idea," Miley said.

"I will be at your side morning, noon, and night—"

"Roxy!" Miley shouted. "Do you want to know what you can do if you *really* want to have my back?"

Roxy stopped her pacing and gave Miley a long look. "I'm listening."

Miley stared down at her Hannah wig, which now resembled a disheveled rat terrier. "It's a good thing Hannah's checking out of this place today," she said. "I only have one wig left."

Once Miley had taken a shower, transformed herself back into Hannah Montana, and finished packing, she and Roxy had gone downstairs to check out and say good-bye to Chad and Jeremy.

The photographer and art director were standing in the lobby, both chatting on their cells. When Hannah walked down the stairs, however, they ended their calls and walked over.

"Thank you again for all your time,"

Jeremy said, taking her hand in his and gazing intently into her eyes. "I'm sure our readers will love the article."

"Oh, they absolutely will!" Chad agreed. "I was looking through the photos last night. We've got some real winners there."

"You do?" Miley eyed them suspiciously. "But what about the time I tripped and got ice cream all over my face? Or when I was tied up by that kite? Or when the wave knocked me down, or when I fell off the boat—"

Jeremy patted her arm. "We were worried, too," he said in a consoling voice. "In fact, I thought I might get fired! Here we were, trying for an elegant and sophisticated Hannah, and what we got instead was, quite frankly—"

"Hannah the Klutz," Chad finished eagerly. "I've never shot a celebrity who had so many accidents. It was really an amazing experience for me."

"Great," Miley said. "Glad I could enrich your life in that way."

"Oh, don't worry a bit," Jeremy said. He beamed at her. "I just got off the phone with our editor-in-chief. The results from our latest reader survey are in. Turns out that the last survey—you know, the one that said readers wanted celebrities to be glamorous?—is completely out of date. Now readers want celebrities to look just like them! Bad hair, bad clothes, bad makeup—*that's* what readers can relate to."

He sighed happily. "Falling flat on your face turns out to be a fabulous career move, and our photo shoot will be on the cutting edge of new celebrity journalism . . . and we have *you* to thank for it! So . . . thank you!"

"Oh. Well. You're welcome." Miley did her best to smile, but she could tell that her best was not very good.

Then Roxy stepped forward. "Don't worry, honey," she said. Although she was talking to Miley, she had moved so close to Jeremy that she was practically nose-to-nose with him.

Her arms were crossed and her expression was stern. "I just *know* Mr. Simple won't make you look foolish in front of his national audience. And you know how I know that? Because Mr. Simple knows that Roxy won't stand for that kind of nonsense. Am I right, Mr. Simple?"

Jeremy's face had paled slightly during Roxy's speech. His eyes skittered around the room, then he nodded rapidly. "Oh, yes, yes, you're absolutely right, Roxy!" he cried. "In fact, I was just chatting with my editor about possible headlines. How does *'Hannah Montana: She's Just Like You!'* sound?"

Roxy lifted one eyebrow and looked at Miley.

Miley thought for a moment, then grinned. "That sounds perfect," she said. "I can't wait to see the issue when it comes out."

Then she and Roxy said good-bye, dashed out the front door, and got into their rental car. As soon as they were far enough from the

Bumblebee Inn, Miley ducked down and pulled off her blond Hannah wig. Sitting back up, she shook out her own brown hair and gave Roxy a high five.

"Ladies and gentlemen, Hannah Montana has left the island," Roxy said as she drove toward the Stewarts' rented summer cottage.

Miley smiled with satisfaction. "And Miley Stewart is officially on vacation!"

# Chapter Eleven

Ah, give me the girl with the bonny
  brown hair.
Your hair of brown is the talk of the town.
    —*"Good Bye, Fare Thee Well"*

The next morning, Miley jumped out of bed, ran to her open window, and took a deep breath of sea air. As luck would have it, her first free day was also a day off for Captain Dan's summer-school class. Lilly and Oliver had already made plans to meet Miley at the cottage and bike over to a beach that was known for good surfing.

The mere thought of what the day ahead

would bring made Miley hum to herself as she went to the kitchen.

"Mornin', sleepyhead," Roxy greeted her. "'Bout time you got up. Lilly called, and she and Oliver are already on their way."

"Excellent," Miley said, pouring herself a bowl of cereal. "I'll eat this real fast so I can start making sandwiches for our picnic." She left the bowl on the counter and opened the refrigerator to get some milk. "Hey, look, leftover fried chicken! Can I take some of that?"

Her dad came in from the deck to refill his coffee mug. "Sure thing," he said. "There's some leftover potato salad, too."

"Great." Miley twirled herself back over to the counter and poured milk on her cereal. She began humming again softly.

"Sure sounds like you're in a good mood, bud," her dad said. "What do you have planned for the day?"

"We're going to take a picnic to the

beach," Miley said. "Lilly wants to surf, of course. I think Oliver wants to use us as bait to help him meet girls and maybe even get a date."

"Best of luck to him," Mr. Stewart said, shaking his head. "Although I think Oliver has about as much chance of getting a date as Uncle Earl has of getting his pigs to sing in a choir."

He took his coffee back out to the deck, where his guitar was leaning against an Adirondack chair. He sat down and called to Miley, "Bring your breakfast out here and let's visit a while."

Miley pushed open the screen door and went outside in her bare feet. She stood still for a moment, staring out at the calm ocean and cloudless sky. "Ahhh," she sighed, taking in the glorious day for a moment before sitting down to eat her cereal.

Her dad sipped his coffee, then picked up his guitar and played a little riff. "So, Roxy tells me you had a rough time on the photo shoot."

"Yeah, I was kind of hoping that someone would accidentally press the wrong button on that camera and delete all the files," Miley admitted.

"I'm sure they're not that bad," her dad said. "And if they are, well, I'm sure your fans will still love you."

"Thanks, Daddy," Miley said. "I think."

She took another bite of cereal just as Jackson wandered over, his hair sticking out at all kinds of odd angles. "What's the matter?" Miley asked. "Couldn't find a comb?" She cocked her head and pretended to study her brother more closely. "No, forget the comb. Looks like you need a rake. Or a Weed Eater."

"It's called 'casually disheveled,' and it's a look," Jackson informed her, punctuating his statement with a huge yawn.

Mr. Stewart shook his head in despair. "It's

hard to believe that a son of mine would have hair like that," he said. As he headed back into the cottage, he added, "Forget gels and conditioners . . . how about just running a hand through your hair?"

Jackson flopped down on a chair and pulled a clump of string out of his pocket. "I would," he called after his father, "but my hands are kind of tied up." He wound the string around his fingers and began making intricate knots.

Miley stopped chewing long enough to say, "What's with the arts-and-crafts project? Now you're doing macramé?"

"It's not macramé!" her brother snapped as he stared down at his hands. His forehead was furrowed with concentration and his tongue was poking out from the side of his mouth as he looped one end of string over the other. "It just so happens that sailors have been doing knot work for centuries to keep from getting bored on long voyages. Yesterday on the boat,

Sam was showing everybody how to do this. Since he's coming over today, I thought I'd see if he could give me a few tips."

Jackson held up his hands and made a face. The string now looked even more messed up than before. "I must be doing something wrong here. . . ."

"Ya think?" Miley asked, but her tone wasn't as sarcastic as usual. Her mind was focused on more important things, like the news that Sam was coming over to hang out with Jackson.

She put her cereal bowl on the ground and stretched out her legs, smiling at Jackson. "So, Lilly and Oliver and I are going to hit the beach today," she said in a friendly voice. "Do you want to come with?"

Jackson gave her a withering look. "Gee, this is so unexpected! To what do I owe the honor of this invitation?"

She nudged him playfully with her foot. "Hey, you're my brother," she said innocently.

"Why shouldn't we have some fun together on vacation?"

"Right." Jackson nodded. "And the fact that I'm hanging with my very good friend Sam today has nothing to do with this."

"Of course not!" Miley said with a forced laugh.

"Uh-huh. Well, sorry to disappoint you, but Sam and I already have plans," Jackson said smugly. "And now I have to get ready."

He sauntered back into the cottage, whistling, just as Roxy came out onto the deck. Miley sank back in her chair, deflated. "Jackson just hates sharing," she complained. "Ever since we were little! First he wouldn't share his blankie, then he wouldn't share his Halloween candy, and now he won't share Sam!"

"Don't you worry," Roxy said. "Remember, I've got your back. And even better, I've got an idea."

Miley's face lit up. "You do? What is it?"

"Never you mind," her bodyguard said mysteriously. "You just leave everything to Roxy."

"Ahh, this is nice," Miley said, stretching out on a towel on the soft, warm sand. She closed her eyes and turned her face to the sky, enjoying the feel of the sun on her face . . . and the cold splash of water on her stomach!

She screamed and jumped to her feet. "Lilly!" she yelled. "That wasn't funny."

Lilly grinned at her. "Yes, it was," she said. "And absolutely necessary. You were going to fall asleep."

Miley sat up and blinked in the bright sunshine. "Okay, you're right, I was," she admitted. "But you could have just nudged me or something."

Oliver had started pulling objects out of his duffel bag and tossing them on his own beach towel: sunscreen, water bottle, snacks, three more Agatha Kilpatrick novels, and a camera.

"I hope you're not planning on using that camera, Oliver," Miley said. "I've had enough photo shoots to last me for ten years."

"Come on, Miley," Oliver said. "It's all part of my master plan. I take pictures of you and Lilly, some other cute girl wanders by, I just happen to get her in one of my shots, I use the opportunity to show her picture to her on the screen, and voila—Smokin' Oken has closed another deal!"

Miley and Lilly both rolled their eyes.

"You just keep telling that story, Oliver," Lilly said. "That's what you're good at."

Miley squinted at the ocean. Waves were rolling to shore in a smooth, steady motion. Sunlight sparkled off the clear water, seagulls wheeled through the sky overhead, and the breeze was scented with the summery smell of coconut suntan lotion.

She glanced sideways at Lilly and Oliver. "Last one in has to buy a round of ice-cream cones!" Then she jumped to her feet and raced toward the surf.

Behind her, she could hear her friends laughing and yelling as they ran after her.

It's so great not to be fretting about my wig anymore, Miley thought as she reached the ocean. Or to be worrying about Chad taking pictures of me.

Although, now that she thought about it, she wouldn't mind if someone had a camera to document this beautiful day . . .

She turned around and saw Oliver pointing his camera at her.

Well, all right! Miley grinned and struck a playful pose.

As Oliver clicked off a few photos, she thought to herself, maybe I'm getting the hang of this after all. . . .

And that's when a wave came up behind her and knocked her flat.

When they had had about all the sun and sand and surf they could take for the day, Miley, Lilly, and Oliver decided to bike back into town for some ice cream. They parked their bikes, got a double scoop each, and wandered along the sidewalk, stopping here and there to peer into store windows.

They had been walking for about ten minutes when Oliver stopped so suddenly in the middle of the block, that Lilly barreled right into him.

"Hey!" she said, staring in dismay at her top scoop—pistachio—now melting on the concrete. "Dude, you officially owe me a cone. What do you think you're doing, stopping like that without warning?"

"Look." Oliver nodded at a large old building across the street. The word LIBRARY was carved in the stone above the door. "That's where we can find the answers that we seek."

"Oliver!" Miley exclaimed. "Why are you talking like a hobbit?"

"I'm not," he said. Then, after a moment, he admitted, "Okay, I am. But only because I just had a thought."

"Alert the media," Lilly said sarcastically. She paused to savor her remaining scoop of chocolate swirl. "Please, enlighten us with your insight, oh brilliant one."

"Your great-aunt Agatha has been a best-selling novelist for years, right?" Oliver said.

Lilly nodded. "So?"

"So, I'm sure there have been a lot of articles written about her," he went on. "And maybe, just maybe, we can find some of them in that library. . . ."

Miley sighed. Here they were enjoying a perfect summer day and Oliver wanted to spend time inside a dark, quiet, library! "Oliver, why do you care so much about Lilly's great-aunt?" Miley demanded.

"Dude!" exclaimed Oliver. "Because she might be—a murderer . . ."

"Listen to this," Oliver said. He read from an article: "'Mrs. Gladys Evans knew Agatha Kilpatrick when the budding author was still writing her first novel. The two women worked together in an office and often chatted during their coffee breaks. "She was pleasant enough, but she made me uneasy," Evans says. "She was always bringing up strange topics of conversation. I remember one time, she asked several of us, 'Have you ever thought about how you would hide a body?' We all thought it was strange. I mean, we just wanted to drink our coffee and maybe brag about our children. But Agatha was always going off on tangents like that.'"

Oliver put the paper down. "See?" he said to Miley and Lilly. "I'm not the only person who's suspected Agatha Kilpatrick of nefarious deeds!"

"I don't know . . . that woman might have just been a very anxious person," Lilly said. "Or very imaginative." She gave Oliver a meaningful look. "Which sounds like someone else I could mention."

Before Oliver could argue, Miley held up her hand.

"I don't know, Lilly," Miley said slowly. "Oliver may be right. Listen to this." She read from a magazine article that she had found. "This is her former college roommate: 'I remember that Agatha used to get ideas for her books everywhere, even when she was doing housework. When she dusted the venetian blinds, she'd start toying with the cord, and then she'd say something like, "This could work . . . maybe Eustace could strangle his uncle who is blackmailing him. . . ." Then she'd pick up a paperweight from her desk and start looking at you in a funny way, and you just *knew* she was figuring out the best way to brain you. It was really kind of spooky.'"

Miley looked up and met Lilly's and Oliver's gazes. "Spooky," she repeated.

"You guys are starting to freak me out," Lilly said. She tried to sound as if she were joking, but she was gnawing her lower lip, a sure sign of worry.

"*Starting* to freak you out?" Oliver exclaimed. "I was at Freak-Out Level Ten two days ago! Listen to this!" He picked up another article and read out loud: "'Agatha Kilpatrick's move to a remote house on Nantucket Island came as a surprise to her friends, family, and publisher. "She said she needed solitude and space for creative inspiration," said her editor, Sarah Jane Parker. "I've only visited her once, but the house is . . . well, *odd* is the best way to describe it, I suppose. She planted a flower bed filled with nothing but poisonous plants. And she talks a lot to her cat—but always in another language, so you have no idea what she's saying. The weird thing is that the cat does seem to understand her. I have to admit, I was quite happy to leave."'"

He lowered the magazine and looked anxiously at Lilly. "Strange. Odd. Spooky," he repeated. "And remember how she warned us against going into that room in the attic? I'm telling you, there's something sinister going on in that house!"

"Oh, come on," Lilly said. "You don't really think there's a body in the attic—do you?"

"Maybe! Could be! In fact, why not?" Oliver said. "That's exactly what would happen in one of her books!"

"Which are *fiction*," Lilly pointed out. "As in, totally made up."

"When are you going to stop denying the facts?" Oliver said loudly.

"Shh!" An older woman who was pulling a book off a nearby shelf glared at them.

"Sorry!" Oliver whispered. He leaned toward Lilly and Miley and whispered, "Listen. All I'm saying is that we should be careful. . . ."

His voice trailed off. His eyes widened.

Lilly and Miley turned at the same time to see what had shocked Oliver into silence. The woman who had shushed them had departed, taking several books with her, and the open space revealed that someone was on the other side of the shelf, watching them. And that person was none other than Mrs. Kilpatrick!

Lilly gasped.

Her great-aunt came around the end of the shelves to greet them. "Well, fancy running into you here," she said smoothly. "I would have thought you'd be spending time on the beach, not inside a library."

"Oh, well, you know how it is," Oliver said, trying to sound casual. "We just love reading! Can't get enough of it! Even when the sun is shining and we're on vacation and you'd think we would want to swim or something—*ow!*"

He glared at Lilly and reached down to rub his ankle.

"We thought we might be getting sunstroke," Lilly said. "We came in here to cool off."

Mrs. Kilpatrick smiled thinly. "Indeed," she

said. "And did you find something interesting to read?"

She glanced at the articles spread across the table.

"No, not at all!" Lilly slammed her magazine shut and shot a wild look at Miley and Oliver. Miley quickly slid her own article into her lap, while Oliver simply sprawled across his, as if he were about to take a nap. "In fact, we were just saying that we should probably get going," Lilly went on.

Her great-aunt nodded, as if this made perfect sense. "Very well. I have a few more errands to run in town, too," she said. "I'll see you back at the house for dinner." She gave them a twinkling look. "I thought we'd have poached salmon and roasted potatoes tonight."

"That sounds delicious," Oliver said.

After Mrs. Kilpatrick left them, he hissed, "Delicious—and deadly! That was what Angela Thorpe-Jones served her husband in *The Corpse in the Kitchen*!"

"Let me guess," Miley said. "Her husband turned out to be the corpse."

He pointed at her. "Bingo."

Lilly was looking worried. "How long do you think she was standing there? Do you think she heard us? What if she tells my mother about what we were saying? Mom told me to be polite and mind my manners, and I can't imagine anything more rude than accusing someone of murder!"

"Technically, we didn't accuse her," Miley said. "After all, we didn't say it to her face."

"No, we said it behind her back!" Lilly countered. "Which is even worse! My mother is going to be so mad if she hears about this."

"Excuse me," Oliver said. "I think you're both missing the point here. Mrs. Kilpatrick was *lurking*. You know what that means."

Miley and Lilly turned identical blank looks on him.

"It means she's guilty!" he said. "Just like the gardener in *Arsenic in the Aspic*!

He lurked. And the butler in *Murder by Marmalade*. He lurked. And the—"

"Okay, okay," Miley said. "Calm down, Oliver."

But Oliver's voice rose in panic. "Think about what she could do to us if she knows we're on to her!"

There was another shushing sound from a corner of the library. He lowered his voice again. "This is a woman who is an expert in poisons!"

The three of them exchanged worried glances.

"The problem is that you don't know anything for sure," Miley pointed out. "She may be a nice old lady . . . or she may be a mass murderer." She shrugged. "Poy-tay-to, poh-tah-to!"

"Yeah. Just keep the jokes coming, Miss I'm-Not-Eating-Salmon-Tonight," Oliver said bitterly.

"Okay, look, we don't have time to have a

fight right now," Lilly said impatiently. "How can we figure out if our suspicions are correct?"

"There's only one way," Oliver said. "We've got to get inside that attic."

Chapter Twelve

Our ship she lies in harbor,
Just ready to set sail.
> *—"Our Ship She Lies in Harbor"*

The next morning, Miley forgot all about the mystery of Great-aunt Agatha when she was confronted with a mystery of her own. Walking into the kitchen, she found a note taped to her cereal box.

"Meet me at the jetty at ten a.m.," it said. "Trust me, you won't be sorry. Jackson."

She frowned suspiciously. Jackson had been remarkably well behaved on this vacation, thanks to all the time he was spending on board the *Trueheart*, learning about mainsails and mizzens. But she knew him too well to relax her guard. He couldn't go for more than a week without pulling some kind of prank. And right now he was long overdue.

Then she saw a P.S. scribbled at the bottom of the note. "I know what you're thinking," Jackson had written. "Trust me anyway."

Miley considered that for a long moment, then shrugged. There was a *faint* possibility that Jackson might be sincere. And there was always a chance she might run into Sam at the jetty, too. . . .

When Miley got to the jetty, however, she was disappointed to find . . . just Jackson. As advertised. He was pacing up and down the jetty and looking annoyed.

Miley sighed. "Okay, Jackson, here I am," she said. "What's up?"

"It's about time!" he said. "My note specifically said 'don't be late.' Can't you read?"

"What's the big rush?" Miley asked.

Jackson checked his watch. "The big rush is that the *Trueheart* is setting sail in ten minutes, and I've got to be on board," he replied. He added, a little cockily, "Captain Dan is giving me a sailing lesson. He said I'm one of the most promising sailors he's ever seen. He said he'll even let me take the helm! He said—"

"Get to the point, Popeye," Miley said. "What does this have to do with me?"

"You'll see." Jackson had a strange little grin on his face. It made Miley uneasy.

She eyed him suspiciously. "Why are you smiling?" Miley asked. "I don't like it when you smile."

"I'm smiling because I'm about to make my dear sister very, very happy," Jackson said solemnly.

Miley's suspicious look deepened. "This better not be a setup for one of your practical jokes, Jackson—"

"Oh, ye of little faith," Jackson interrupted. "You'll see, pretty soon you'll be nominating me for Brother of the Year."

He glanced over her shoulder, then added quickly, "And listen, one more thing. Remember that guys don't always come right out and say what they're feeling. You've got to get better at reading between the lines, okay?"

Miley gave him a puzzled look. "Jackson, what is going on? You're sounding even weirder than usual, which I didn't think was possible."

"Never mind, you can thank me later," Jackson said. Then he waved at someone behind her and yelled, "Hey, Sam!"

Miley whirled around to see Sam jogging up to them. He was wearing a blue T-shirt, faded khaki shorts, and sneakers. "Hey. Sorry I'm late." He glanced at Miley, then looked away quickly, his face growing redder. "Um . . . hi, Miley."

"Hi," Miley said, her eyes darting back and

forth between Sam, who was staring at his feet, and Jackson, who was grinning as if he had just given her the best birthday present in the world.

"Since I'm going to be Captain Dan's second mate today, Sam has the day off," Jackson explained. "Roxy wanted to do something special for you—I guess she feels she owes you a favor or something?—so she arranged for Sam to take you on a sailboat ride."

"Oh." Miley's face went blank. She quickly grabbed Jackson and pulled him aside.

"Wow. This is great, Jackson. Thank you," Miley whispered to him. "But how did Roxy convince you to help out?"

Jackson shrugged. "I guess she figured that I wouldn't turn down a chance to be second mate," he said, grinning. "Especially since Tanya, Clarissa, and Samantha are going to be on the crew."

In the distance, a ship's bell began clanging.

"I've gotta run!" Jackson cried. "See you later!"

As Jackson dashed off, Miley turned back to Sam. To her surprise, he was looking at her—in fact, he was actually making eye contact!

"Let's go," he said. "It looks like a great day for a sail."

And indeed it was. Miley was astonished to find that once Sam was sailing, his distant manner with her totally disappeared. She didn't notice this right away, of course. For the first thirty minutes, she was too busy trying to keep her balance and follow Sam's instructions to pay attention to anything else.

But as soon as they were on the open sea, with only a few other boats in the distance, she was able to relax. She sat next to Sam, who was steering the rudder with one hand while pointing out interesting sights with the other.

"See that beach?" he said. "When I was eight years old, I was swimming about fifteen yards offshore and a shark brushed right past me. This close! Scared the daylights out of me."

"It would have scared more than that out of me," Miley said. "What did you do? I've read that if a shark attacks you, you're supposed to punch it in the nose. Do you think that would really work?"

Sam grinned. "Not if he was really hungry! Anyway, by the time I realized what had happened, the shark was already halfway to the horizon. Still, I was shaking for about an hour." He glanced up at the sail. "The wind's shifting from the southeast," he said. "I'll just tack her over so we can head for the point. If we're lucky, we'll see some dolphins today."

"That would be awesome," Miley said.

Miley soon forgot that she had ever stressed out about Sam not talking to her.

As they sailed, Sam talked about the history of Nantucket. He talked about the whaling ships that used to sail from there in the nineteenth century. He talked about the best time of the year to see whales, how proud he was to work for Captain Dan, and his dream of sailing around the world in a tall ship someday. He seemed, in other words, exactly the opposite of the quiet guy who couldn't look Miley Stewart in the eye.

"You really love sailing, don't you?" Miley said finally.

"How can you tell?" he asked with some surprise. Then he seemed to replay everything he had been saying for the last half-hour in his head, and he laughed sheepishly. "Sorry. I've been talking your ear off."

"No, no, not at all," she protested. Then she caught his eye and started laughing, too. "Okay, maybe a little bit. But I was interested, really."

"Well, I do feel more at home on the sea than anywhere else," Sam admitted, adjusting the rudder slightly. "Duck!" he yelled as the boom swung around.

Miley ducked, and the boom cleared her head by mere inches.

"Sorry I didn't give you more warning," Sam said. "The wind's picking up. I think we should head for the cove. It's one of my favorite places."

"You mean *another* one of your favorite places," Miley joked. Sam had already told her that a certain beach, a particular pizza place, and a specific bike trail were his favorite places.

"I'm glad you're keeping track," Sam said, giving her a sideways glance.

Miley looked at Sam as he watched the horizon, his profile etched against the summer sky. "You seem so different today," she told him. "I mean, different from when you were—"

"On dry land?" He finished her sentence with a grin. "I know, I know. I have kind of a hard time talking to, um"—he shot her a quick glance, then looked away—"well, to people. But out here, it's different. When I'm out on the water, I feel . . . free."

As the little boat leaped over the waves, Miley leaned back, closed her eyes, and enjoyed the feel of the wind in her hair and the occasional drops of sea spray on her face. The sun was warm, but not too hot, and she felt a wonderful sense of complete relaxation.

"I know what you mean," Miley said. And then somehow, because the feel of the speed and the wind and the sun made her feel reckless and bold, she dared to add, "I'm glad. I was afraid you didn't like me."

There was a slight pause. Miley's heart thumped. She couldn't bear to open her eyes. Why, oh, why had she said that?

Of course he was just taking her out as a favor to Jackson.

Of course he didn't really like her—at least, not in a flirty, romantic way.

And, of course, she had now ruined what had been turning out to be a perfect day.

Why couldn't she leave well enough alone! Now he would really hate her. . . .

And then she heard him say, with great assurance, "I like you fine, Miley. In fact, I think it's one reason I've been even quieter around you."

Okay, that didn't *sound* like he hated her. . . .

Miley felt a small flicker of hope. She cautiously opened her eyes. Sam was smiling at her, a warm, friendly smile that seemed to make the whole world shine.

"Oh," she said, relieved. "Good. Because, um . . . I like you fine, too."

By the time they reached the cove, the sun was setting. Sam lowered the anchor, and they sat together, watching the last of the golden sunlight spill across the waves.

Above them, the night sky was a clear, deep blue with just a few stars visible yet. The sailboat rocked easily on the waves, which slapped gently against its hull.

Sam heaved a sigh and stretched his arms

above his head. "I can't believe summer's going to be over in, what, like, three weeks?" he said. "And then school will start . . ." He shuddered dramatically.

Miley imagined herself starting school back in Malibu. Three thousand miles away. "I know," she said with a sigh.

Then she noticed the bracelet on his wrist. "Hey," she said, "that looks like what Jackson was trying to make the other day."

"Oh, yeah, I was teaching him how to make a Turk's head bracelet," Sam said. He slipped his off and handed it to her.

"Turk's head?" Miley asked, turning the bracelet over in her hand.

"Yeah, it's just a braid that's woven into a circle," he said. "Sailors used to make these on long voyages for their sweethearts."

Miley twirled it around her finger. "Nice," she said.

"Well, they had to pass the time somehow." Sam said.

Miley just looked at him. "Uh-huh."

"Come on," he said. "They were at sea a long, lo-ong time!"

"Right," she said.

He grinned. "Okay, I know what you're thinking and you're right," Sam said.

"Oh, yeah," Miley asked teasingly. "What am I thinking?"

"I can try to explain it six ways from Sunday, but you want to know the truth?" Sam said. "Those guys just *loved* doing macramé."

Miley started giggling. She couldn't wait to repeat this to Jackson!

"Anyway, I like to keep the tradition alive," Sam went on. "It makes me feel connected to the past somehow, and all those sailors on those whaling ships."

"Kind of like singing sea chanteys," she said, tossing the bracelet back to him.

Sam shook his head. "Oh, man," he said. "You're going to go back to Malibu and tell everybody you met the biggest nerd in the world—"

"The Nerd of Nantucket." Miley giggled. "No, really, I think it's so cool that you've figured out ways that you can be a part of history, in a way. And I loved hearing you sing sea chanteys the other night."

Sam rolled his eyes. "I used to only sing those at home with my parents and their friends," he said quickly. "Captain Dan was the one who got me to sing in public. He said the tourists would love it and they do. But believe me, I'd never do it if Captain Dan didn't ask me to—"

"Hey," Miley said, putting a hand on his arm. "You don't have to explain. You've got a great voice, why shouldn't you sing for people?"

Sam looked embarrassed but pleased. "Well, thanks," he finally said. "I have to admit, when we're out in the middle of the ocean on the *Trueheart*, and I'm singing a chantey, and I imagine sailors singing the same words on the same kind of ship over a hundred years ago, well it's kind of. . . ."

He paused, as if trying to think of the right word.

"Magical," Miley said.

"Yeah," he said softly. "That's exactly it. Magical."

For a few moments, they just sat quietly, enjoying the silence of the night.

Then Miley finally spoke up: "How did that 'A Hundred Years' song go again?" She hummed the tune softly.

Sam began singing, and, after a moment, Miley joined in. By the time they reached the chorus, they were belting out the words as boldly as pirates. Then they came to a rollicking finish:

A hundred years is a very long time,
Ho, yes, ho!
A hundred years is a very long time,
A hundred years ago.

The echoes of their voices drifted across the

water and gradually faded away. Miley smiled up at the stars above them. Suddenly, one of the stars fell from the sky, streaking toward the water with a silver flash.

"Quick, make a wish," she said. She closed her eyes and made her own private wish, crossing her fingers for extra luck. When she opened her eyes, Sam was smiling at her.

"Well?" she asked. "Did you wish?"

He looked away. "Um, yeah," he muttered.

Miley's heart sank. Oh, no . . . had the shy and practically wordless Sam returned?

Before she could get too upset, though, he turned to look her in the eyes. "Hey, if you like falling stars, you should come on our Meteor Shower Cruise tomorrow night," he said. "Captain Dan does it twice a year. Sometimes you can see dozens of falling stars in an hour." He paused, then added, "That's a whole lot of wishes. . . ."

"Thanks, Sam," Miley said, beaming. "I'd love to."

Chapter Thirteen

Cape Cod cats ain't got no tails;
Haul away, haul away;
They lost them all in northeast gales.
　　　　　　—"Cape Cod Girls"

Oliver lay in bed, his covers pulled up to his chin, and stared wide-eyed at the ceiling.

Not that he could see the ceiling, of course, since his room was shrouded in darkness. The heavy velvet curtains were closed, the hall light had been turned out, and he didn't even have the comforting glow of a digital clock. Instead, an old-fashioned windup alarm clock ticked away on his bedside table.

In the complete and utter silence that

enveloped the house, the clock's ticking sounded ominously loud. It almost sounded like a heartbeat, Oliver thought.

Like the heart of a murder victim perhaps . . .

A heart that had been hidden somewhere in this sinister house of secrets. . . .

A heart that wouldn't stop beating until its desire for revenge had been satisfied!

Oliver had read a short story in school that had a very similar plotline. It had made a big impression on him.

He squeezed his eyes shut and noticed that his own heart was thumping as well. And that's when he heard the soft squeak of his bedroom door being pushed open. . . .

"*Aaee.*" He tried to scream but only managed a strangled squeak.

"*Shh!*" The door closed, and a flashlight flicked on, revealing Lilly dressed all in black. "It's me."

"Don't you know how to knock?" Oliver tried to sound testy to make up for his pathetic little squeal.

Even across the room, he could hear Lilly sigh in frustration. "Why should I knock when you were supposed to be expecting me?" she asked impatiently. "We said we'd rendezvous at midnight, and it's twelve on the dot. Now come on, let's go."

Oliver threw back his covers and got out of bed. He was still wearing the jeans and T-shirt he'd had on all day. As he knelt down to search for his sneakers, he said, "You know, I've been thinking . . ."

"Oh, boy," Lilly said. "Here we go."

Oliver didn't like her tone. He didn't like it one little bit.

"What?" he asked defensively.

"You always do this, Oliver," Lilly hissed. "You come up with some crazy scheme and you get your friends to agree to go along with it, then you have"—she made air quotes with her fingers—"quote, unquote, 'second thoughts' and try to back out last minute."

"You know, Lilly, sometimes second

thoughts are good things," he said stiffly as he felt under the bed. "Sometimes they mean that there's a little voice inside your head that's whispering, 'Maybe we shouldn't do this.'"

"*You* were the one who said she might be hiding something sinister!" Lilly whispered. "*You* were the one who said we had to find out the truth!"

"Well, now I'm thinking that I was wrong," he said weakly. "My mom gave me all these rules about being a good house guest. Say thank you, offer to do the dishes, remember to hang up your wet towel. I'm pretty sure that she'd think breaking into a locked room and looking for dead bodies is kind of rude."

"And getting killed in our beds would be kind of stupid," she snapped.

"Hey, you were the one who said I was making a big deal out of nothing," Oliver said. "And you know what? You were right."

Lilly took a deep breath. She was about to

utter words that had only passed her lips a few times in her life . . . and never while she was talking to Oliver.

Slowly, she let the breath out and squinched her eyes shut. "No, Oliver," she said in a strangled voice. "I was wrong."

Oliver's mouth dropped open. "What did you just say?" he gasped. "You can't be serious!"

"Look at me Oliver!" she snapped. "Do I look like I'm serious?" Lilly held her flashlight under her chin. The light cast weird, ghoulish shadows over her face.

Oliver shuddered. "That is *so* not a good look for you."

"Focus!" Lilly hissed. "We may be alone in a house with a murderer!"

"*Eee*," Oliver squeaked again and put his hands over his ears.

Lilly dropped the flashlight and pulled his hands down. "Or not," she went on. "Either way, we need proof. I'm going up to the attic, with you or without you."

"Okay, okay," Oliver said. He glanced down at the flashlight and followed its beam straight to his sneakers, lying under a pile of dirty clothes.

Somehow, it seemed like a sign.

Oliver sighed. He was a big believer in signs. He put his sneakers on.

"All right," he said to Lilly. "I'm ready. Let's go."

Fifteen minutes later, Oliver and Lilly had only made it halfway up the staircase to the attic. Each time Oliver took a step, the wood under his foot would creak, his heart would start racing wildly, and he would freeze in place. Then Lilly would poke him in the back. Hard. As they got closer to the top of the stairs, the creaking only sounded louder, his heart pounded harder, and Lilly's pokes got more and more painful.

Oliver paused, took a deep breath, and eased his right foot onto the next step.

Carefully, he put his weight on it.

Ahh. His shoulders relaxed. No creak. No poke. Maybe he was getting the hang of this. . . .

"Hurry up!" Lilly whispered. "We don't have all night."

"You wanted me to lead the way," he reminded her. "Let me lead!"

He took another wary step.

Oops. That was a very loud creak.

Ouch. And a very pointed poke.

He whipped his head around to glare at Lilly. "Stop it!" he hissed. "I'm going to have a bruise if you keep doing that."

"You're going to have more than a bruise if you don't get a move on," she said.

"Fine!" Oliver walked up the last few steps and halted in front of the attic door. Now his heart was hammering so hard that he thought he might faint.

He put his hand on the knob and slowly turned it, halfway hoping that it would be locked and they could simply go back to bed. Besides, if Mrs. Kilpatrick was hiding evidence of her crimes in this room, surely she'd be smart enough to lock the door. . . .

No such luck. The knob turned easily. Oliver pushed the door open as slowly as he could. Then he and Lilly quickly slipped into the attic and shut the door behind them.

It was a large room, but it felt tiny, thanks to the many objects that crowded the space. A dressmaker's dummy stood in one corner and seemed to watch their movements with disdain. Several rickety tables, piled high with everything from a huge birdcage to an aquarium filled with broken seashells to stacks of old newspapers, were shoved under the window. A rack of old, moth-eaten clothes stood against.one wall. Another whole wall was filled with tilting towers of cardboard boxes and piles of dusty, ancient books.

Lilly and Oliver spent a few moments poking around but found nothing except a small mouse who was not happy about being disturbed.

Once Oliver got down from the chair he had jumped onto when the mouse ran squeaking by, he decided he'd had enough. "Well, nothing to see here," he said brightly to Lilly. "Race you downstairs!"

She shot him a disdainful look. "Are you kidding? We haven't even gotten started. There are at least a dozen places to hide a body. I'll look in this trunk. You look behind that rack of clothes."

Oliver gingerly approached the lineup of old coats and limp dresses. They smelled strongly of mothballs. He focused his mind on trying not to sneeze.

Then he froze. Maybe it was just the movement of the air now that he and Lilly were walking around, or maybe his footsteps on the wooden floor were sending up vibrations, but the clothes began to sway on the rack. To Oliver's overheated imagination, they looked like dancing ghosts.

He backed away a few steps and glanced over his shoulder at Lilly. She, of course, was already kneeling by the trunk and lifting its lid without hesitation.

Oliver scowled. Sometimes he wished Lilly weren't quite so intrepid. She set a standard that was very hard to match.

Lilly sat back on her heels. "Nothing here but a bunch of old photos," she said. "What about you?"

When he glanced back at the clothes rack, his heart skipped a beat. Had they moved some more when his back was turned?

His knees shaking, Oliver edged closer. Only the thought of Lilly, standing behind him and watching, made him plunge his arm between a musty tweed overcoat and a faded housedress.

He felt around with his hand, his eyes squeezed shut in dread, and touched . . . the wall.

Oliver sighed with relief. "There's nothing here," he said. He pulled out his hand and patted his shoulder as if he were congratulating himself. "Well, I guess we can head downstairs now—"

"Wait." Lilly was staring past him with a determined look in her eyes. Oliver felt the hairs on the back of his neck rise up. He had seen that expression on Lilly's face before, when she took on a champion skateboarder in the finals of a half-pipe competition. He knew what that look meant. Lilly wasn't giving up.

"Really," Oliver went on, without much hope, "I think our work is done."

But Lilly narrowed her eyes and shook her head. "There's one more place we haven't searched," she said in a hushed voice. "It looks like a closet. . . ."

Lilly pointed to the far end of the attic. Sure enough, there was another door, half-hidden by a broken coatrack and the bottom half of a suit of armor. Briefly, Oliver wondered how Mrs. Kilpatrick had come to own a suit of armor—and where was the top half of it? He didn't have time to give these questions much thought, however, because Lilly was already marching toward that door, and she clearly expected Oliver to be right behind her.

Oliver had seen far too many horror movies to let his friend leave him behind and open the mysterious closet door alone. The character who marched bravely forth on her own always ended up being the first victim, usually within the first fifteen minutes of the movie.

Oliver might feel very, very, very annoyed with Lilly right now, but she was still one of his best friends. He wouldn't let her die alone.

So he crept up behind her and held his breath as she reached out her hand, hesitated for a second, then jerked the door open . . .

Oliver opened his mouth, but he had

finally reached a point where he was too frightened to scream.

Grinning down at them with a maniacal gleam in her eye was . . . Mrs. Kilpatrick!

Chapter Fourteen

Our anchor we'll weigh, our sail we will set,
The friends we are leaving, we'll never forget.
*   —"Good Bye, Fare Thee Well"*

"*Aaaaahhhhh!!!*" Once Oliver got over his initial shock, he found his voice again. His scream was just as loud as Lilly's, just as heart-felt, and perhaps even a little higher.

He grabbed Lilly, remembering from his knowledge of horror movies that victims who could run fast sometimes got away. He tried to pull her back, but Lilly just screamed again at the feel of him clutching her shoulders.

He vaguely remembered from hours of

watching horror movies that the jock character would sometimes run away in a moment like this, leaving his or her less athletic friends behind to die. And Lilly was the fastest runner he knew.

Well, he wasn't going to let her abandon him! Oliver grabbed her.

Lilly screamed again. Then she glared at Oliver and elbowed him in the stomach.

"*Oof!*" Oliver grunted and doubled over, shooting Lilly a betrayed look. He might have still had a chance to escape! But now, thanks to his *former* best friend, that chance was gone. The only thing left to do was die with dignity. . . .

He heard what sounded like clapping and cautiously opened one eye. It *was* clapping . . . in fact, Mrs. Kilpatrick was applauding!

She saw him looking at her and nodded cheerfully. "Congratulations to you both," she said warmly. "That was very well done."

"Wha-what was?" Lilly asked, her voice quavering.

A look of concern passed over her great-aunt's face. "Oh, dear, you're both shaking," she said. "Let's go downstairs and have a cup of tea. I'll explain everything."

As they descended the stairs to the kitchen, Oliver managed to find a moment to whisper in Lilly's ear. "If we're killed tonight, I just want you to know this is all your fault!"

Lilly waved a hand at her ear, as if brushing off a fly. "Yeah, whatever," she said. "Like I'll even care once I've been murdered!"

But once they got to the kitchen and Mrs. Kilpatrick turned on the lights, put the kettle on, and took a package of chocolate cookies out of the pantry, Oliver began feeling . . . well, if not at ease, at least less frightened.

Then Mrs. Kilpatrick poured them each a cup of tea. Lilly and Oliver sat for a long moment, staring down at their drinks, then they looked up at the same instant and met each other's eyes.

Mrs. Kilpatrick began laughing. "Oh, dear,

I'm so sorry," she said. "But you should see the look on your faces! Here, I'll drink first, how's that?"

She took a sip of tea, then smiled over the rim of her cup. "See? Still here, still breathing."

Lilly pushed her cup away. "Caffeine keeps me awake," she said.

"Ah." Her great-aunt nodded solemnly, but her eyes were twinkling. "Well, I'll just enjoy my own tea, then." She took another sip, still chuckling slightly. "Oliver? What about you?"

Oliver felt that it was high time to take control of this situation. "Maybe I'll drink my tea," he said, "once I know what the joke is."

Mrs. Kilpatrick nodded and put her cup back in its saucer. "You're quite right, I should explain everything," she said. "Well, as I told you, I do a great deal of research for my books. The one I'm working on right now, for example, involves a poisoning. The murderer uses the root of a rare wildflower—"

Oliver gave Lilly an "I-told-you-so" look, which Mrs. Kilpatrick intercepted. "Yes, I saw you pick up on that when I brought my little bouquet in from the garden," she said. "Very clever of you!"

Oliver beamed with pride before he remembered that he had just been scared out of a year's growth. "Well, it wasn't hard," he said. "You had mentioned jimsonweed at breakfast, and I remembered that. It didn't seem important at the time, but—"

"But later it made you wonder!" Mrs. Kilpatrick cried. "Exactly! That's the key to every mystery! The small, seemingly unimportant fact that turns out to be a vital clue—and, of course, someone smart enough to notice it and put all the pieces of the puzzle together!"

She gave Oliver a look of such warm admiration that he blushed. "Thanks," he said. "I've learned a lot from your books, of course—"

"Oliver!" Lilly snapped. "Aren't you forgetting something?"

There was a silence while he thought about this. "What?" he asked.

Lilly tilted her head toward her great-aunt. "You know."

His confusion deepened. "I do?"

Before Lilly could get angry enough to throw something at him, Mrs. Kilpatrick stepped in.

"What Lilly is trying to say is that you both suspected that I was a murderer," she said calmly. "Which was just as I planned."

Lilly's mouth dropped open. "You planned—"

"Everything," her great-aunt said calmly. "You see, I'm working on a new mystery novel that includes two characters who are still in high school. In fact, they're the main characters. When they realize that something is amiss, they do all the detective work to discover the guilty party. But it's been so long since I've spent time with teenagers. I just wasn't sure how my characters would really react if they were placed in a strange situation"—she waved one hand—"such as this house. Or how they would deal with a seemingly batty old woman who appeared to have a mysterious secret."

Oliver suddenly saw everything that had happened over the last few days—the dinner conversation about poisons, the warnings not to go in the attic, the deadly flower bouquet—in a totally new way. "You *wanted* us to be suspicious!" he cried. "You wanted to see what we would do."

"Exactly." Mrs. Kilpatrick looked quite smug as she finished her tea. "And I must say, you've given me some wonderful ideas. Looking up articles about me in the library—that's a whole new chapter!"

Lilly was beginning to smile. "So that's why you were lurking behind the bookshelves," she said. "You were following us."

"Actually, I was there to check out a few

books on ancient Sumerian daggers," her great-aunt admitted. "That's for the next novel, I think. Although"—she got a distracted, distant look in her eyes—"I wonder whether Cecily *really* would find the dagger in Jonathan's trunk? Could he have kept it hidden for all those years . . . hmm, perhaps I could . . . no, that won't work . . . unless I establish that Jonathan has invented a new kind of padlock. . . ."

"Aunt Agatha!" Lilly said loudly. "You were spying on us in the library, weren't you?"

"What?" Mrs. Kilpatrick seemed to suddenly remember where she was. "Oh, yes, of course I was. When I saw you come in, I decided that I simply had to eavesdrop a bit. And then I kept an eye on you when you were here, too." She raised one eyebrow. "After all, I wasn't sure how long it would take two young people to break their solemn promise to never, *ever* go into a certain attic. . . ."

Great-aunt Agatha gave Lilly and Oliver a

stern look over her glasses. "I had originally thought that it would take at least a month for my characters to crack, which was causing me endless problems with the timeline. I'm so relieved to find out promises only last a few days."

Lilly and Oliver blushed.

"Okay, that wasn't our best moment," Oliver said. "But remember, we *did* think you were a killer."

"Fair enough." Mrs. Kilpatrick got up and began rummaging through a drawer. She pulled out a battered notebook and a pencil and dropped back into her chair.

"Now, why don't we have some more tea, and you can tell me exactly what you were thinking and feeling as you climbed the stairs to the attic." She flashed them a pointed smile and added, "I hope you don't mind if I take notes."

Chapter Fifteen

In the morning bright and early;
Won't you go my way?
In the morning bright and early;
Won't you walk my way?
　　　　—"I Met Her in the Morning"

On their last night on Nantucket, the Stewarts and Roxy booked passage on Captain Dan's Midnight Meteor Shower Cruise. Mrs. Kilpatrick bought tickets for herself and Lilly and Oliver, explaining that she felt she owed them something for the terror she had put them through.

The passengers met on the dock and boarded the *Trueheart*, which had Christmas lights strung along the railings and among the sails. Captain Dan welcomed everyone and told them to enjoy the food and drink that had been set up on a table in the stern.

Miley spotted Sam moving toward her through the crowd. "Hi," she said shyly.

"Hey," he said, smiling. "I'm glad you could make it."

"Me, too." Miley tilted her head back to look at the mast, twinkling with lights. "Great decorations."

He laughed. "Thanks. It took me all day, but it's worth it. Come on, let's get something to eat."

"You don't have to work?" Miley asked, surprised.

"I gave him the night off," a gruff voice said behind her.

She turned to see Captain Dan holding Roxy's hand. Miley's eyes met Roxy's, and they shared a secret smile.

"Part of the night off, that is," Captain Dan

continued. "The boy's still gotta sing for his supper."

"Glad to," Sam said agreeably. "And speaking of supper—"

He grabbed Miley's hand and guided her to the back of the ship. They filled their plates with food while the crew cast off and the *Trueheart* headed for open water. As they left the lights of the town behind, Miley felt a wave of pure happiness sweep through her.

"Dude!" Suddenly a loud voice interrupted her perfect moment. Miley made a face before turning around to see Jackson's goofy grin. He chuckled at her expression and clapped Sam on the arm. "This is totally awesome! Hey, do you think Captain Dan would let us climb in the rigging tonight?"

"Not a chance," Sam said. "Too dangerous."

"Danger? Ha!" Jackson cried. "We laugh at danger."

Sam grinned and Miley felt her heart sink.

It was just like Jackson to try to worm his way into their conversation. And after he had been nice enough to set up that wonderful afternoon sail with Sam . . .

Just as she felt her stomach twist with jealousy, she saw Roxy threading her way through the crowd toward them.

"Jackson, I've been sent over here to give you a message from the captain," she said in an official-sounding voice.

Jackson straightened up as if he were about to salute.

"Captain Dan wants you to take the wheel until it's time to drop anchor," she said. Then she winked at him. "And Samantha asked if she could be your first mate."

Jackson's face lit up with glee. "Really? Gee, thanks, Roxy!" He turned to Sam. "Sorry, dude. Catch you later."

"Yeah," Miley echoed as Jackson hurried off. "Thanks, Roxy."

Her bodyguard grinned and leaned over to

whisper to her. "As I said before . . . Roxy's always got your back!" She gave Miley a little salute and sauntered back to where Captain Dan was waiting.

After they had sailed for almost half an hour, the *Trueheart* stopped and dropped anchor. Captain Dan stepped up onto a wooden box and whistled for everyone's attention.

When they had all quieted down, he smiled and thanked them for coming. "We should start seeing our meteor shower in an hour or so," he said. "So, while we're waiting, I thought you might all enjoy hearing some songs that sailors sang a century ago." He waved to Sam. "Sam, come on up here!"

Sam stepped up onto a box to the sound of light applause. "This is one of my favorites," he said. "It's called 'I Met Her in the Morning.'" He paused, then began to sing in a clear voice:

I met her in the morning;
Won't you go my way?
I met her in the morning;
Won't you go my way?

In the morning bright and early;
Won't you go my way?
In the morning bright and early;
Won't you go my way?

I asked that girl to marry.
Won't you go my way?
I asked that girl to marry.
Won't you go my way?

She said she'd rather tarry.
Won't you go my way?
She said she'd rather tarry.
Won't you go my way?

Oh, marry, never tarry.
Won't you go my way?
Oh, marry, never tarry.
Won't you go my way?

Together, the passengers joined Sam as he sang the verse again, then they burst into loud applause. Sam sang several more songs as Miley stayed in the back of the crowd, smiling and clapping along. At some point, she realized that her father had come up behind her.

"So, what do you think, bud?" he asked. "Was it a good vacation?"

"The best," Miley said.

"Hmm." Her dad nodded toward Sam. "I'm guessin' you'd like to tarry a bit yourself."

"Oh, well, you know," Miley replied, blushing. "Maybe just a little."

He patted her shoulder. "That's all right, darlin'. Just as long as you don't decide to go away anytime soon."

"You know I won't," Miley said, giving him a hug.

"Good," he said. "Now, why don't you take that Sam a soda. He must be mighty thirsty after all that singing."

A short time later, Captain Dan turned off the running lights to make it easier to see the meteor shower. The ship rocked gently on the waves, engulfed by the dark of the water below it and the star-spangled sky above.

Miley had walked forward to the ship's bow, where she stood above the figurehead and stared into the night. A sense of sadness played at the edges of her mind. It was hard to believe that this week was already over. It was even harder to believe that, just when she'd gotten to know Sam, she'd soon be boarding a plane and flying back to Malibu.

A slight breeze lifted one brown curl off her forehead. She smiled and closed her eyes. This wasn't a time for sadness. It was a time for enjoying the feel of the cool air and the sound of the waves lapping against the side of the ship.

Someone touched her shoulder. She turned to see Sam standing behind her. "Are you having a good time?" he asked.

"I'm having a wonderful time," she said. "It's beautiful out here."

Miley gazed at his dimly lit face, trying to memorize the moment. She could hear the other guests talking and laughing softly in the rear of the boat. Still, she almost felt as if she and Sam were completely alone.

Then there was a collective gasp from the guests behind them. Sam looked past Miley's shoulder and nodded.

"First falling star of the night," he said.

Miley turned to look at the sky. "Darn, I missed it!" she said. "There goes my wish."

"Just wait," Sam said softly into her ear.

Sure enough, a minute later another star streaked through the sky. Then another and another.

Sam put his arm around Miley, and together they stood in silence, watching. After some time, Miley let out a small sigh.

"Is something wrong?" Sam asked.

"I'm just a little sad that I have to leave

tomorrow," Miley said. "That's all."

"Me, too." He cleared his throat, as if embarrassed by his admission, and quickly added, "But I brought something for you."

"You did?" Miley turned to him.

"It's nothing, really," Sam said, looking even more bashful. He held out a small circle of braided rope. "Just a little souvenir to make sure you remember Nantucket."

She slipped the bracelet onto her wrist. Then she smiled at him. "Thanks," Miley said. "But don't worry. I don't think I could ever forget it."

Acknowledgments

Special thanks to Captain Dow, Mitchell Waters, and the Disney Press editorial team.

About the Author

Suzanne Harper has written two novels for teens, *The Secret Life of Sparrow Delaney* and *The Juliet Club*, as well as several nonfiction books, numerous magazine articles, and several plays. She earned degrees in English and journalism from the University of Texas at Austin and a master's degree in writing from the University of Southern California. She lives in New York City. You can visit her at her Web site, www.suzanneharper.com.

Check out the first original story!

ROCK the waves

by Suzanne Harper

ed on the series created by Michael Poryes and Rich Correll & Barry O'Brien

Ride the wave
Summer sun, summer fun, summer love
Ride the wave
Let it bring you what you're dreaming of

The sun had already risen high in the cloudless blue sky over Malibu by the time fifteen-year-old Miley Stewart woke up. She pushed a strand of brown hair out of her eyes and blinked sleepily at her bedroom ceiling, sensing that there was something different—something delightful—about this morning. The only problem was that she couldn't quite remember what it was.

Two birds sang sweetly to each other in the jacaranda tree outside. She turned her head toward the window, smiling, then realized that this was the first thing that was different: she could actually *hear* the birds. Usually, the gentle sound of birdsong would be totally drowned out by the painful sound of her older brother, Jackson, singing loudly and incredibly off-key in the bathroom.

She lay still for another moment, luxuriating in the sense of peace and watching dust motes dance lazily in the sunlight that slanted through the window curtains.

Then she stretched her arms over her head, enjoying the feeling of being completely rested and relaxed . . . which, now that she thought about it, was also strange. Usually, every morning started with her desperately trying to find the braying alarm clock so she could hit the snooze button one more time. . . .

That was it! Her alarm clock hadn't gone off! Miley bolted out of bed, panicky, and raced to her closet. She should have known as soon as she saw the way the sunbeams crossed her room that the sun was higher in the sky than usual, which meant that it was very late, which meant that she would probably miss the first bell, which meant . . .

She stopped abruptly in the middle of the room as she finally remembered the glorious fact that had been nagging at her since she first woke up.

No, she wasn't going to be tardy. Because *this* was the first day of summer! Three months of fun and friends and freedom stretched out in front of her, like a glorious present waiting to be unwrapped!

Miley did a little dance of joy before running out of her room and down the stairs.

"Good morning!" she called out to her father, who was mixing pancake batter in the kitchen.

"Well, someone's in a good mood today," Robby Ray Stewart said teasingly. "Hmm. I wonder why that is?"

"Because I'm free," she said happily. "Free, free, free!"

Miley skidded to a stop and reached over the counter to put a finger in the bowl of batter. "Free," she repeated dreamily one more time as she licked her finger.

"Whoa, there, bud, you can lick the bowl *after* I've finished making pancakes for everybody," her father said.

"But there won't *be* any batter left after you've made the pancakes," Miley pointed out reasonably. She snuck her finger in the bowl again. "Yum."

"Mornin'." Jackson, Miley's brother, wandered into the kitchen. His tousled dark blond hair made it clear he'd just stumbled out of bed. So did the fact that he was still wearing pajama bottoms and a T-shirt. Yawning, he grabbed a plate and held it out to his dad. "The pancakes smell great. I'll have five, please. No, seven. Actually, I'm starving, so how about eight. . . ?"

"Whoa, whoa, whoa," Mr. Stewart said. "Don't you want to take a gander at my works of art here first?"

Miley rolled her eyes. Her father had grown very proud of his ability to create what he called "picture pancakes"—batter poured to resemble objects and animals—and insisted on asking his children to identify them before being served.

Unfortunately, trying to figure out what the pancakes were supposed to be wasn't always that easy. Mr. Stewart would claim that the pancakes were alien spacecraft or giraffes or pickup trucks, but they all looked like blobs to Miley. Tasty blobs, but blobs nonetheless.

Jackson peered suspiciously at the skillet. "Oh, man. Is that a tarantula? You know I hate eating anything that looks like a spider."

"Now, why in tarnation would I make a tarantula pancake?" his father asked testily. "Look closer."

Jackson tried again. "An octopus?"

"No! Open your eyes, boy!"

Jackson's stomach growled. His hunger drove him to start making wild guesses. "An amoeba? A sailing ship? A car engine?"

"No, no, and no." His father flipped the pancake, looking hurt. "It's a palm tree! I can't believe you couldn't see that!"

"Oh, yeah, *now* I do," Jackson said, hoping to get back in his dad's good graces—and get some breakfast—as soon as possible.